Beach House Wedding

by

CORA SETON

More by Cora Seton

Beach House Romance
Beach House Vacation

For my husband, Lennard.
I love you.

CHAPTER 1

October

"TODAY'S THE BIG day?" Emma Hudson asked.

"Today's the big day," Penelope Rider confirmed. "My first guests are arriving at EdgeCliff Manor." She made a face. "I swear I'm going to mess up and call it Fisherman's Point at least once while they're here."

"You'll do fine," Ava Cross said.

The three women had met up moments ago in the Cliff Garden, the beautiful one-acre property attached to Emma's bed-and-breakfast, Brightview. They'd waved to Emma's sister, Ashley, who was hard at work weeding, and started their usual walk toward the beach.

Summer had faded into fall, but in coastal California, that just meant the skies were a brilliant blue, the fog had disappeared and the days were as warm as ever. Plenty of guests still wanted to visit. Penelope knew Brightview would be packed this weekend, and it sounded like the Blue House, Ava's vacation rental, was booked, too.

Their beach houses stood in a row on Cliff Street,

perched high on the bluffs overlooking the Pacific Ocean. They'd each inherited a home within the past year, a coincidence that had thrown them together from the start and made them feel more like sisters than friends. Ava's house was in the middle, and Pen's at the far end, closest to Sunset Beach. Their morning walks led them either along the bluffs or down to the sand where they could walk in the surf. Some mornings Emma's golden retriever, Winston, joined them, but today Winston had gone with Emma's husband, Noah.

Penelope was in a hurry. She still had a lot to do before she welcomed her guests this afternoon. EdgeCliff Manor needed to be spotless. She needed to arrange fresh flowers in all the rooms, make sure there was new soap and shampoo in the bathrooms, pick up fresh ingredients for snacks, and a hundred other last-minute details.

She intended her first private wedding to go off without a hitch. After all, who knew when she'd get a chance to host another celebrity.

"I wonder what Olivia Raquette is like in person?" Ava asked. With her athletic build and penchant for exercise clothes, Ava always looked to Penelope like she was about to call everyone to order and start a yoga class. Her auburn hair was pulled into a sensible ponytail this morning.

"Do you think she'll sing at her own wedding?" Emma chimed in. Blonde and cheerful, Emma went in more for sundresses and sandals.

"Do you think she'll do that dance?" Ava asked with a mischievous grin.

Olivia Raquette was "internet famous." She was a singer who had gone viral at eighteen after posting a high-quality video of herself doing a very salacious dance while belting out a very salacious song. Penelope had done some reading up on her and found out her family were old-money Boston bluebloods, and Olivia had used part of her trust fund to entice a well-known director to create the video for her—all with the tacit approval of her parents, as far as Penelope could tell. That same money had bought her the kind of behind-the-scenes know-how it took to make sure her video went "viral." Now she had a music career and a rabid following—and she was getting married. Penelope wondered privately if everything was as fabulous as Olivia's social media accounts portrayed it to be. After all, the young star had jumped at a chance for a small, discount wedding at an untested venue that only held forty guests for the ceremony and reception, and a maximum of twenty overnight if people were comfortable with very close quarters. Wouldn't a real star want something far bigger?

"She asked for a very boutique, upscale wedding," Penelope told them. "A string quartet is coming to play at the ceremony and for the couple's first dance."

"That seems totally out of character for her." Since Penelope had booked Olivia, all three of them had become experts on the star, and it wasn't unusual for Penelope to hear Olivia's music playing at her friends' houses when she stopped by to chat.

"Maybe," Penelope said, "but she comes from New England old money, so maybe it's not unusual at all if you consider her background. Maybe understated is the way they do everything."

"I don't know," Ava said. "Seems a little fishy to me."

Penelope repressed a pang of unease. She needed this wedding to go off without a hitch. It had occurred to her, too, that Olivia could be pulling some kind of publicity stunt, and the thought left her heart pounding. What if the whole thing was a joke and she ended up looking like a fool for being part of it? Was it true that all publicity was good publicity? She hoped she didn't have to put the old saying to the test.

They arrived at the steps leading down to the beach. "I need to keep this walk short today," Penelope told her friends. "Let's stay up here, okay?"

"That works for me," Ava said. "I need to get to work early. I'm taking my class on a field trip today."

"Sounds good." Emma led the way down the wide sidewalk instead. Cliff Street was a favorite place for people to walk. Once you passed Penelope's house, the view of the ocean was unobstructed for the rest of its length as it wound along the top of the bluffs. Later in the morning, it would be thronged by tourists and locals, and even now there were plenty of people around. Surfers wanting to get some time in the waves before work. Joggers and power walkers who wanted to beat the crowds.

"By the end of the day there'll be ten people staying at my house. Olivia is bringing them all to help set up. What do you think they're going to do for nine whole days? The wedding isn't until next Saturday."

"Are you nervous?" Ava asked.

"Very," Pen admitted. "This is my first time hosting guests, my first wedding party, my first everything. What if it all goes wrong?"

"It'll be fine," Emma assured her. "We'll be ready to help with anything you need. Besides, Olivia's wedding planner is handling most of it, right?"

"That's right. Amber is in charge. I'll be her right-hand man."

"Woman," Ava corrected her. "What's Amber like?"

"Driven. She's not actually a wedding planner at all. She's Olivia's manager, and she seems to be in charge of everything Olivia does." They made their way around a jogger who'd stopped to re-tie his running shoe. "She's like a drill sergeant. She keeps sending me checklists a mile long."

They walked a few moments in silence before Emma asked tentatively, "Are you up for this, Pen? These people sound picky."

"I still don't understand why you two don't run your

vacation rentals like I do," Ava added. "My business is almost totally hands-off. My guests show up, I give them a key and that's it until they leave."

"Unless you decide to marry one of them," Emma teased her. Ava had fallen for one of her guests, Samuel Cross, a few months back, and they'd married over Labor Day. She turned back to Penelope. "This wedding sounds like a lot of hard work."

"It's everything I hoped for," Penelope said. "This is exactly why I renovated Fisherman's Point—EdgeCliff Manor," she corrected herself. "So that fancy people could hold their exclusive, fancy weddings here. You haven't told anyone it's happening, have you?" she added, suddenly worried one of them might have let something slip. She was supposed to keep everything confidential until the big day, according to the paper-work she'd signed, but Ava and Emma were her closest friends.

"I haven't breathed a word to anyone, not even No-ah," Emma said. She'd gotten married in July. Penelope was sad she hadn't been able to host either of her friends' weddings, since she'd still been fixing up her house, but since Emma and Ava both had their own beach houses, they didn't need her services, anyway. "Not that Noah even knows who Olivia Raquette is," Emma added.

"I haven't told Sam, either," Ava said. "I'm afraid he *would* know who she is and might mention it to Ben."

Ben was Sam's business partner, who would be relocating to Seahaven in the spring. "I can't control what Ben says to anyone."

"Good. Thanks for keeping it a secret." Penelope breathed easier. She was a little intimidated by Amber Bentwick. Penelope had the feeling the woman was going to run her ragged. She had already mentioned the need for a few "alterations" to the house and deck. Pen had assured her she could handle the work, even though she had no idea what the scope of it would be. She kept telling Amber she and her "crew" could accomplish anything that was necessary, but she hadn't confessed that she was her own crew and she'd done all the renovations to the house herself, with the help of a cousin now and then when she really needed a second pair of hands.

"When it's over, you can finally take that boat your uncle left you for a spin," Emma said. "You can go fishing and relax."

Penelope glanced out at the ocean, every fiber of her body craving a day at sea. "You're right. That's something to look forward to." She hoped her friends didn't notice the strain in her voice. She hadn't taken out the *Amphitrite* since she'd inherited her uncle's fishing charter boat along with the house. Hadn't been out on it for months prior to his death, either. Her relationship with her uncle had been difficult toward the end. She knew she'd disappointed him deeply and was fairly certain she'd inherited the house and boat only because he hadn't had time to change his will before his sudden death from an aneurysm last fall.

Once she'd thought he'd be proud to pass his fishing charter business to her. After all, she was the one who'd run it for him on the many days in the last few years he'd woken up too stiff or hungover to do it himself. She was the one who'd served his guests their breakfasts, outfitted them with the gear they needed and herded them down to the marina and onto the boat. She was the one who'd brought cup after cup of black coffee to her uncle and chivvied him down to the *Amphitrite*, as well. She was the one who'd gotten the motors running and steered them out to fertile waters. She'd guided the customers, coaxing and flattering them into casting and reeling in with enough skill to actually land something—all the while making them think they'd done it themselves.

She was the one who'd mopped up vomit when a customer proved unseaworthy and didn't make it to the railing. She kept the tall tales flowing about past fishing trips and unlikely catches, making the guests laugh when their spirits were dipping.

She'd brought them back to port at the end of the day, made sure the gas tanks were full, docked the boat and got it shipshape for the next day's trip. Then she'd gutted the catch and either cooked it or prepared it to send home with the clients, and she'd done it all with a smile on her face.

All that counted for nothing in the end.

One mistake had made her uncle banish her forever. Now the house and the boat were hers, but the thought of taking the *Amphitrite* out to sea left her cold with dread. The loss of her uncle had wrenched her heart in two.

The loss of his respect had devastated her.

She needed cash to keep her new home, however, so Penelope had decided to be practical. She renovated Fisherman's Point. Rebranded it. Turned it into a boutique wedding venue she knew would draw a profit—as soon as people found out about its existence.

Meanwhile the *Amphitrite* sat in its slip. Penelope visited it there, spending time tending to it, telling herself her uncle would approve of that much, at least. She dreamed of the business she once thought she'd spend a lifetime running. She could feel the wind in her hair, the wheel under her hands. She knew where the fish were. Longed for a fishing rod to hold—and to share her love of the sport with others.

Still, she couldn't bring herself to take the boat out. She kept hearing her uncle's voice—his roar of disgust and disapproval when she'd tried to board the *Amphitrite* late last summer. She'd hoped enough time had passed that he'd forgiven her for what had happened, but she was wrong. He'd still been furious.

And then he was gone.

Sometimes Penelope wondered if she'd been fooling herself all along. Maybe Uncle Dan had always wanted a son. Maybe he'd accepted a niece as a poor substitute, and when he'd finally realized it wasn't the same thing at all, he'd cast her off because he'd thought he had time to find her replacement.

It turned out he didn't.

Now the legacy she'd thought was her due weighed on her like a judgment. She should sell the *Amphitrite* if she wasn't going to use it.

But she couldn't bear that either. Not while the sea still called her.

Penelope shook off her unhappy thoughts. She had to get real. There was no fishing charter business anymore. There was no Fisherman's Point. She was about to premier her small, elegant wedding venue, and nine days from today she'd host her first major event. This was her life now.

Everything else was just a silly dream.

"I have some news," Emma said, jolting Penelope back into the present. "I'm pregnant."

Ava whooped and hugged her. "That's fantastic news!"

"It is," Penelope said more slowly, still half-buried in worries about her own future. "How far along are you?"

"About two months. We were supposed to wait for three months to tell anyone, but I couldn't stand it anymore. Noah agreed we could spill the secret."

"I'm so glad you did. You must be so excited," Ava said.

"I am. I'm really happy!"

Penelope hugged her, too. "Well, I'm thrilled. I know how much you wanted a baby."

"You two need to catch up. I want our children to play together." Emma hugged them both back.

Ava beamed at her, but Penelope felt the smile slip from her face. She didn't have a boyfriend let alone a husband, and she was in no financial position to have a child on her own.

Emma and Ava didn't notice that she hung back as they kept walking. Penelope trudged behind them.

When would her life turn around?

"I'LL BE THERE in ten days," Westin Abbott, Wes to his friends, said into the phone as he made his way to airport security.

"That's not good enough," his father, George Abbott, said. "We need you here now. This is an emergency."

"I notified you of this trip a year ago," Wes pointed out. He scheduled all his fishing vacations well in advance to steer clear of problems. His parents resented the time he spent away from the company, but it was the only thing that made it possible for him to work there at all. Wes had never wanted the job as VP of Sales at Abbott Enterprises and had shown little aptitude for the day-to-day details. Aside from his parents, everyone was happier when he was gone. His deputy VP, Dexter Stone, appreciated it most of all, since it clarified to the rest of their team who was really in charge.

"We've let you skate your way through life this far. Now the bill has come due. Did you really think we'd pay you an executive's salary for doing nothing forever?"

"I never asked you to do it in the first place."

"You never turned down the cash, either," his father snapped.

Wes wasn't going to touch that with a ten-foot pole. He was putting his salary to work in the best way possible, as far as he was concerned.

"What's the crisis? You need me to sweet-talk someone?" That was his one strength. Wes might steer clear of Abbott Enterprises as much as possible, but he always came home for the events his parents threw several times a year. He was great at working a crowd.

Three years ago, when the crucial Danielson contract was slipping through their fingers, Wes had cornered Edward Danielson himself at their annual holiday bash. They'd talked about China's competition in the industry, the rise of solar power usage in rural Ghana, the propensity of college women to change their majors—Danielson had three daughters at Princeton—and Danielson's fears that the back injury he'd sustained recently would keep him from ever playing tennis again.

It was this last subject they'd really drilled down on.

Wes asked a dozen questions about how Danielson had been injured and how he felt now. He asked Danielson if he'd consulted an expert in sports medicine directly and gave him the name of a friend in the field. He asked what Danielson himself thought the healing process would look like, and they went through possibilities step by step.

Wes did none of that out of a desire to manipulate his family's potential customer—he did it because he was genuinely curious. His parents never seemed to understand that when he tried to explain how he "worked his magic," as they called it. There weren't any tricks to explain.

He liked people.

All of them.

"We need you to take your sister's place as CEO," his father said.

Wes stopped in his tracks, the river of fellow passengers flowing around him. "What did you say?"

"You heard me. Grace is out. You're in. So get home, now."

Wes stepped to the side of the wide hallway and tried to process his father's words. Grace was the golden child in their family. The one who'd done everything right as far as his parents were concerned. She'd aced her way through business school, gotten her MBA with flying colors and worked her way up swiftly through the company until she'd taken over day-to-day operations to let their parents rest on their laurels a little.

Now they were firing her?

"Why?"

"Because we need you." His father's exasperation was clear.

"Why is Grace out of the company? What happened?"

There was a long silence, uncharacteristic of George Abbott. "No need to get into that over the phone. It's serious, though."

Wes didn't believe that. His parents and Grace must have had a spat. Maybe she was making a play for more autonomy in the way she ran the company. It had always struck Wes as strange that his parents wanted her to take the reins so early. His mother and father were still young. Still loved to micromanage every detail of the operations. Why were they always pretending to be retired when they were anything but?

"You're going to have to be more specific." He hadn't talked to his sister since the last time they'd passed in the halls of Abbott Enterprise's New Jersey headquarters. As usual, she hadn't hidden her scorn, and Wes hadn't lingered to ask her questions about her personal life.

"Let's just say she got greedy. She's out," his father repeated. "When are you coming home?"

Home.

The word made Wes shake his head. The large penthouse condo his parents occupied had never been home to him, even if they did keep a bed for him to use when he was in town. Wes liked to think of himself as a vagabond. He sent his mail to a PO box. His business wardrobe lived in the spare room of his parents' place. Everything else he owned—his camping equipment, skis, golf clubs and other items he only used now and then—were kept in a storage locker. The rest fit in a backpack or suitcase—or happened online.

"I don't want to be CEO," Wes said. "I'm not interested in telecommunications. I have no aptitude for managing people. Find someone else."

Another pause. "Westin Abbott, you listen to me. We were there for you when you needed us. We bailed you out when *your* company went under and you were about to default on that stupid loan you accepted from your *friend*." His father's emphasis on the final word of that sentence made Wes's stomach twist. His friend had turned out to be connected to all the wrong people.

"I know," Wes growled. "I've thanked you for that." He'd been twenty-two. Stupid. Eager to show his parents he wasn't the waste of space they'd always thought he was. He'd already proven he didn't have what it took to succeed at Abbott Enterprises, so he'd started his own business, his first attempt at being a fishing guide. He'd bought a boat with the help of Kennedy Mayor, a loud-mouthed braggart on his rugby team who was always flashing cash around. Kennedy was supposed to be his partner in the scheme. When it turned out the boat was a lemon, in constant need of repair, and Wes didn't know the first thing about running charters, he'd quickly gotten in over his head.

Shame still burned through him when he thought about the way it had all fallen apart. His dad had bailed him out—

And then never let him forget it.

"That was over a decade ago," he said now.

"And you've taken every handout I've given you since."

"Because you asked me not to take another job." God forbid he embarrass his family by going to work for a lesser business—and failing at that, too.

"You are an Abbott. You work for Abbott Enterprises—full time. No more trips. Starting now."

"I can't."

"What do you mean you can't?"

Wes's explanation died in his throat. How could he tell his father he was ready to try starting a fishing charter business again? He'd hoped to keep it under wraps until he'd succeeded. He couldn't afford to fail twice.

"I'll be back in ten days," he said again. "We can discuss things then. I'm about to get on my plane."

"Wes—"

He hung up and tried to shake off his foreboding. Surely by the time he got back to New Jersey, his folks would have patched things up with Grace. No sense getting too worried until he saw for sure this was a problem that wouldn't go away on its own.

Wes focused on getting through security. Only when he was seated in the departure area, watching planes take off and land on the tarmac, did he allow his thoughts to return to the subject.

Why did this have to happen now when he was so close to his goal of opening his charter business? This time he'd saved up cash to fund it himself, living frugally while banking the generous salary he got from his parents. His one expense was his frequent fishing trips. He'd spent the last decade learning about being a guide from some of the best around. His last few vacations had been scouting expeditions of a sort. He was having a hard time choosing a location to base his operation out of. His sole criteria was that it be far, far from New Jersey, which didn't whittle the possibilities down very much.

Had his father somehow sensed he was about to make his escape?

Wes must have sighed, because a cute blonde sitting across from him raised her gaze from her phone.

"It can't be a long day yet," she said. "It's only nine a.m."

He shrugged, pulled out his phone and tapped on a random app. The blonde returned her attention to her own screen. He wasn't looking for companionship right now. No entanglements. He had far too much going on for that, and he wasn't going to change course now—for a woman or for his parents. Should he contact Grace directly and find out what this was all about?

He hesitated before deciding against the idea. He pulled up a news site instead and scanned the business headlines. When he saw no mention of Abbott Enterprises, he decided his father must be yanking his chain, trying once more to see if he could force Wes to take a more active interest in the company.

Six more months, he told himself. In six months he'd have enough money saved to buy a fishing boat outright, plus enough left over to last a year or more as he established his business. After this trip was over, he planned to stay in New Jersey through the Christmas party season, work potential clients for his parents' firm, go to charity events and spread goodwill in the Abbott Enterprises name, then collect his usual year-end bonus. That would bring his savings high enough for the boat. Continuing to work through April would garner him enough to plump up his emergency fund.

Everything was on track.

Eight hours later, on the opposite side of the country from where he started the day, Wes found his rental car at the San Jose airport and stored his luggage in the trunk. His father had left a half-dozen messages, each more insistent than the last one that he come straight home. Climbing into the driver's seat, Wes answered his phone when it rang again.

"I can't come home," he said in anticipation of his father's demands.

"You're in California?"

"That's right." His father must have looked up his email about the trip.

"Fine," he growled. "You have until Monday." He hung up.

Wes put the phone away and started the car. There was no way he was heading home early. He'd looked forward to this trip all year.

He didn't need directions for this drive. He knew the road to Seahaven by heart. As he pulled out, he wondered again what Grace had done to get his parents in such a snit. It must have been bad if they were asking him to replace her. How could they think he'd fill her shoes, anyway? It was ridiculous. He couldn't take over a business he had no interest in.

He'd never been the son his parents wanted.

Wes took a deep breath. He had to shake off this bad mood. Despite what his father had said, he had a glorious ten days of fishing ahead of him. Seahaven and Fisherman's Point were as familiar and comfortable to him as an old flannel shirt, more of a home than his family's sterile condo.

At least some things never changed.

THIS WAS GOING to be a disaster.

Penelope watched a limousine struggle to fit into the

parking area between her house and Cliff Street. Olivia Raquette and Amber Bentwick had to be in the back seat, along with the rest of Olivia's entourage. What were they saying right now? Did Olivia hate the place? Was Amber scrambling to find them alternative arrangements?

Three vans were still in the street, evidently waiting their turn to try to wedge into the small parking lot, too. That must be all the gear for the wedding. Amber had insisted she'd handle everything.

Penelope took a deep breath, opened the door and stepped outside, waving her hands to get everyone's attention.

"There's more parking down the street. You'll have to take turns unloading," she called when the window of the first van rolled down and a man poked his head out. "Down the street," she called again. The man shook his head, revved his engine and swerved around the tail of the limousine before driving away. The other vans followed.

When the limousine finally fit diagonally across the parking area, boxing in her CRV, a man got out, opened the back door and helped two women to their feet.

"Look at this!" one of them said as Penelope approached. She gestured to the awkward parking arrangement. "Why didn't you warn us you couldn't accommodate a limousine? Didn't that seem like a pertinent piece of information?"

"Y-yes." Penelope put a hand out to shake hers. "I'm Penelope Rider. Owner of EdgeCliff Manor. Welcome. A-are you the bride?"

She realized how stupid the question was the minute she asked it. Of course this wasn't Olivia Raquette. The young girl—woman, Penelope told herself—standing beside her had to be. She recognized the internet star's face, although nothing else about her looked the way she normally did online.

"I'm not the bride," the older woman snapped, ignoring her hand. "I'm Amber Bentwick."

Penelope pulled it back. "Of course. Excuse me— the excitement has my tongue twisted up. You're Olivia," she said to the younger woman, who was dressed in cutoff army pants, Chuck Taylor high-tops, a tank top and her hair hanging lankly around her shoulders. Was she aiming for a retro grunge style? Hadn't she been a redhead in her last video? Now she was platinum blonde. "It's so nice to meet you. I'm a big fan."

Olivia rolled her eyes.

"Come in." Penelope didn't know what else to say. This wasn't how she'd expected their introductions to go. "Let me show you around."

"Ugh," Olivia said. Not waiting for another invitation, she flounced past Penelope, up the steps and into the house.

"Right. Let's get started. We've got lots to figure out." Amber followed Olivia, pulling out her phone and tapping at it. "We'll begin with the ceremony. There will be fifty-two guests."

"Forty," Penelope exclaimed, rushing after her into the house. She followed Amber down the central hall. "You said forty guests." Behind them she heard a babble of voices and looked back to see the rest of Olivia's entourage carrying luggage into the house.

Lots and lots of luggage.

She told herself not to worry about it and focused on Amber again. Olivia's manager had stopped, turned and was now looking at her so disdainfully she might as well have said aloud, "I'm dealing with an amateur." Heat rushed into Penelope's cheeks. She snapped her mouth shut and told herself she could handle an extra twelve guests.

"Fifty-two guests," Amber repeated. She pivoted on her high-heel clad foot and kept going to where the hall opened into the great room at the back of the house. It encompassed a kitchen, dining and living room area, with a view of the Pacific Ocean. Olivia had flung herself across the nearest sofa, knocking an embroidered pillow onto the floor. Penelope had made it herself, back when she'd had time for crafts. The young woman stared out the floor-to-ceiling windows as Amber paced around the room. "Next order of business, where to stage the ceremony. Olivia, inside or out?"

"These doors fold away." Penelope rushed to show them. She demonstrated with the nearest one, pushing it open until it fitted into the wall, making the living room and deck all one contiguous area.

"Olivia?" Amber said. "Should the altar be inside or outside?"

"Stop asking me questions!" Olivia's already high-pitched voice threaded upward into something approximating a wail. "I'm tired. I'm hungry. I'm sick of questions! I'm sick of you and everyone else!"

"Chelsea!" Amber snapped her fingers, and an assistant appeared, a young woman whose dark hair was pulled into a barrette high on her head and who had a phone in her hand.

"Seltzer water, lime, Ibuprofen, cool compresses, pajamas, bed."

"On it," Chelsea said. "Olivia, come with me, and we'll make you perfectly comfortable."

"I'll never be perfectly comfortable again!" But the diva allowed herself to be led away and taken upstairs.

"Show me the rest of the house," Amber said as if nothing had happened. "I want to see every detail."

She was a woman of her word. Amber opened every closet as they moved through the first floor of the house. She looked in every cupboard, inspected every windowsill and piece of artwork on the walls.

Finally she gave a long-suffering sigh. "These finishes aren't what I expected from your website at all."

"They're exactly as listed," Penelope said firmly. Granted, when Amber and Olivia had first seen the website, she'd had only computer renderings of what the house would look like when it was finished, but she'd switched them for photos each time she'd finished a room over the last couple of weeks.

"Still." Amber's disappointment was plain to see. "We have a lot to do. That has to go, certainly." She pointed to a large oil painting done by a local artist that Penelope had splurged on. She loved the painting—a scene of the Seahaven harbor, boats shrouded in an early morning fog. There was such a sense of anticipation to it. You could tell in an hour the fog would clear, people would make their way to their boats, a wonderful day on the water would start…

Had Amber ever been fishing?

Penelope doubted it.

"Where do you want the plants?" a man yelled from the front door.

"Plants?" Penelope repeated.

"I knew your landscaping would be hopeless," Amber said. She raised her voice. "Come around the side of the house through the gate."

Penelope looked past her to the yard beyond the deck, where she had planted a few flowering shrubs with help from her friends, Kate and Aurora, who ran a landscaping business. "But—"

"We are throwing the wedding of the century," Amber snapped. "It's going to be perfect. Do you have a problem with that?"

"No." She couldn't have a problem with it. She needed this wedding. Needed the ridiculously low fees she'd earn by hosting it, since she'd given Olivia a steep discount in order to capture her business. Needed the publicity she'd garner even more.

She'd spent everything she had. If Fisherman's Point—EdgeCliff Manor!—didn't turn a profit, fast, she was toast.

"All of this has to go." Amber waved a hand at the furniture Penelope had painstakingly chosen from catalogs and nearby stores with help from her friends. She'd been so relieved when it had been delivered and she'd placed it around the huge room. She thought it looked fantastic, but Amber's lip curled as if she'd just caught sight of a ratty armchair left at the curb.

"Go where?" Penelope asked.

"Wherever you put your extra things." Amber sniffed, clearly losing patience fast.

Penelope didn't have any extra things, but she figured she could arrange for a storage container if she really needed one. Could she do it quickly enough to suit Amber?

"We'll move it for you," Amber huffed as if assuming this was the problem. "Just give me the keys to your storage."

"I'll have to find those for you." Penelope took out her phone, opened a note app and tapped out a reminder, mostly to give her a way to avoid Amber's disgust.

"Oh, for heaven's sake. Charlie?" Amber called. "I need all of this gone. Find a place to put it. She doesn't have any storage." She waved a hand to encompass the living room, kitchen, deck—possibly the whole house, Penelope thought.

"The deck furniture is—"

"Atrocious," Amber cut her off. "Look. You did your best. I can see that. Olivia Raquette requires more than that. She requires the very best that anyone can offer. You're down here." Amber held her hand parallel to the floor at waist level. "She's up here." She raised her hand above her head. "You can't even comprehend her needs. That's what I'm for."

Penelope swallowed. "Sure. Whatever." Tears pricked at her eyes as she thought about how she'd pored over magazines to discover what furniture and patio equipment graced the luxury houses featured in their pages. How had she missed the mark so badly?

"I know this is all new to someone like you," Amber said, not entirely unkindly, which made it worse somehow. "We'll be transforming this space. It's what we do everywhere we go. Olivia is photographed all day long. That's her job."

Penelope had thought singing was her job, but maybe that was simply the excuse for the photographs. The young woman was certainly beautiful to look at—when she'd washed her hair.

"We create the illusion that Olivia's entire life is a

dream. Got it? Nowhere is a dream," Amber said. "Not until we get our hands on it. Off you go." She made a little shooing motion, flashing Pen a smile that disappeared the minute a row of workers streamed into the house. "No, you can't bring those in here yet," she called out and strode away to talk to a man who was carrying a large cardboard container.

Penelope slipped past them to the central staircase and darted up two flights of stairs to her third-floor suite. She was thankful to shut the door on the frantic activity on the lower floors, but as soon as she did, despair overtook her. This was never going to work. If Amber didn't like the furniture and deck accessories, she was going to hate everything about EdgeCliff Manor.

Worse, if Amber was going to transform the place, Olivia's wedding photos wouldn't look anything like the house people would find if they tried to book EdgeCliff Manor for their own events in the future.

She'd overreached herself. What did she know about weddings?

Penelope flopped back on her bed.

One thing was for sure, everything had already gone so wrong, it could only get better from here.

"Penelope?" Amber's voice wafted up the stairs and through the door to her apartment. "Can you come down here? We need to consult about your electrical panel."

Her electrical panel? "Coming," Penelope shouted

back. She sat up wearily. It was going to be a long nine days.

WHEN HAD FISHERMAN'S Point gotten a new coat of paint?

Wes slowed his rental car to a crawl along Cliff Street as the big old beach house came into view. For as long as he remembered, it had been a sort of tannish color with darker brown trim. Hideous, really, as every self-respecting fishing lodge ought to be. Now it was a creamy confection, and Wes felt as disconcerted as he would if someone had dolloped cake icing on a bowl of clam chowder.

What had possessed Daniel Teresi to gussy up his house like this? Had the old bachelor finally gotten married? The thought of it made Wes's heart sink.

He told himself it was just a coat of paint, but Wes was relying on his vacation at Fisherman's Point to be exactly the same as it always had been. That last call from his father had weighed on his mind the whole drive over. Somehow his attempt at a compromise was more disconcerting than any of his previous demands had been. George Abbott never compromised. Which meant this problem with Grace might be more serious than Wes had thought.

His second hint that something was very wrong came when he tried to pull into the gravel parking area behind the house and found it already full. Three vans and a CRV filled the space, since the vans were parked haphazardly. The house had a number of rooms, and it wasn't unusual for at least one more party—sometimes two—to be in residence at the same time he came, but the parking area was spacious. He'd never had to find a spot on the street before.

By the time he'd done so and dragged his luggage back to the house, Wes was thoroughly out of sorts. This had to be the end of the indignities, he told himself. As soon as the door opened, Fisherman's Point would be exactly the same as it always was. He'd settle in his spartan room, grab a beer from Dan's well-stocked fridge and join the other guests on the back deck for a drink before turning in. Dan would tell some funny story about how the house's paint color had come to change. They'd have a good laugh, swap some fishing tales and that would be that.

The door opened before Wes could knock, however, and a teenager spilled out of it, yelling, "I hate herbal tea. Why are you always trying to force herbal tea down my throat?" She was wearing what looked like pajamas, although it wasn't remotely dark out. Her bare feet sported fuchsia-colored nails.

"Your voice is your instrument," an older woman said, hurrying out the door behind her. "You need to treat it like a Stradivarius violin."

"Since when do violins drink herbal tea?" The younger woman came to a stop. "Who the hell are you?"

Up close, Wes could see she was slightly older than he'd first thought, closer to twenty, the kind of gloomy, too-skinny waif that always seemed to be in vogue. The woman following her, cup of tea in hand, didn't seem too pleased with the role of den-mother. She had a brittle, driven look Wes recognized from the female VPs at his parents' business. The kind of woman who was far too smart for the confining role she was forced to play while biding her time to move on to bigger and better things. He'd bet there was a streak of fury lurking under all that officious competency.

Before Wes could answer, a third woman hurried out of the door. She stopped when she took in Wes's suitcase, and a wary look came over her face. He could almost see her pull herself together and accept a new challenge to add to an already challenging day. This woman was beautiful in a wholesome way. Lush dark curls framed her face. She looked professional and lovely in a linen skirt and white blouse. She lifted her chin, came down the steps and approached him.

"Hello. I'm Penelope Rider. And you are?"

He had no idea how Penelope Rider was linked to Dan. She was far too young to be his wife, unless the old man had gotten lucky in all kinds of ways. Was she a relative? Wes racked his brain. Had Dan ever mentioned his family?

"I'm Wes Abbott. I have a reservation."

Penelope's mouth dropped open. The older, brittle

woman laughed. "Like hell you do. We've booked this house until next Sunday." She turned on Penelope. "Right?"

"That's right. EdgeCliff Manor is all yours."

EdgeCliff Manor? Was this one of those gag shows? The kind where unsuspecting people were pranked for the enjoyment of the audience?

Wes had always hated them.

"I have a reservation at Fisherman's Point," he said loudly, all the frustration of a long day's travel catching up to him at once. "Where is Dan? He'll sort this out."

Understanding flashed over Penelope's face, followed by something like pity, before she got control of her emotions and arranged her expression in a business-like manner.

"Amber, Olivia, why don't you head out back to the deck? The view is so restful, you'll find all your stress slipping away. I'll get Mr. Abbott sorted out, and we'll talk more about where the string quartet should go."

"You'd better take care of this... *problem*... quickly." The older woman gave Wes a scathing look before corralling the younger one and marching her inside. As soon as the door was closed behind them, Penelope turned back to him.

"Uncle Dan died last year," she said with no preamble. "He left his paperwork in an awful jumble. I went through everything and called all the clients who had bookings. At least, I thought I did. I'm so sorry I missed you somehow. I don't remember seeing your name at all."

"I have a standing reservation." Wes was reeling from the information. Dan, dead? "He probably never wrote it down. What—did he die from? He couldn't have been more than sixty." Wes couldn't fathom a world in which his old mentor and friend didn't exist. Dan had filled in more gaps in his knowledge of the fishing world than anyone else. He'd encouraged Wes to work toward a day when he could run a charter of his own.

"He was fifty-seven," Penelope said. "He had an aneurysm. Got out of bed one morning and dropped like a stone, from what we could tell. One of his fishing clients found him."

"You're related to him?" It was the shock of the news after a long day of traveling, he told himself. That's why he felt like someone had hit him with a two by four. He was dizzy, suddenly, hot and cold, a sheen of sweat forming at his hairline.

"Yes, I am. Hey, you'd better sit down." Penelope guided him to the steps and sat down beside him on the concrete. "Are you okay?"

"I didn't know… I thought he was still here." Wes waved a hand to encompass what he was feeling. He didn't normally get emotional, but he'd been depending on Dan's warm and offhand hospitality. He thought of the man as part of his family, in a way. Dan was a dinosaur. He didn't have an online booking system, and he didn't own a cell phone. You called his landline, booked your dates and just showed up.

"I'm sorry," Penelope said again. "I wish I'd known you had a reservation." Worry pinched her pretty face. "Like Amber said, I booked the whole house for Olivia's wedding. Olivia is the young woman in the pajamas who was out here when you arrived."

"Is she old enough to get married?" he managed to joke, though talking suddenly felt difficult. It was as if his words were caught in his chest with his thumping heart.

Dan was gone? How was that possible?

Penelope laughed. "I guess so. She looks about fourteen, doesn't she? Doesn't stop her from being a complete tyrant. I'm scared of her. But I'm even more afraid of Amber, her handler." She swallowed. "Sorry, I shouldn't be babbling at you. You've had a shock. You said you've been to Fisherman's Point before?"

"Every year for ten days. I arrive the first Thursday of October and stay through the following Sunday."

She nodded. "That explains why I've never met you. I usually take a two-week cruise with my mom in early October. Until this year, anyway. Otherwise we would have met before. I worked with Dan for years."

Wes stared at her, trying to take this in. Penelope knew Dan far better than he had. She'd been mourning him all this time—and taking over his business, by the looks of things.

"So you're running the fishing charter business now?" Could this woman really step into Dan's shoes? He wasn't sure how he felt facing a week of fishing with her. He'd run into female guides before, of course, but they'd been middle-aged, sun-worn and capable. Penelope looked far too fresh-faced. Besides, she wasn't Dan. He came to spend time with the man as much as he did for the fish.

A flush crept up her cheeks, and her gaze dropped to the ground. "I re-tooled the business," she said after a pause. "I'm doing boutique weddings these days."

And Wes finally understood. Amber's words sank in. The sulky little diva—Olivia—had booked the whole place for her wedding. They would fill the house with puffy dresses and veils and cakes and stupid flowers for the rest of the week. There wouldn't be any comfortable nights on the back deck. No grouchy early mornings when the dregs of the previous day's drinks left you heavy and clumsy until the fresh ocean breeze blew the cobwebs out of your brain and the sunshine perked you up for another round of fishing. There wouldn't be the thrill of the tug on your line or the frustration of losing your catch at the last minute. There wouldn't be any of Dan's hearty dinners or hour after hour of tall tales and salty wisdom.

"You sold his boat?" The thought of it made him green around the gills. The *Amphitrite* was a hell of a vessel, the kind of boat Wes ached to own. If he'd inherited Fisherman's Point, he wouldn't have changed a thing. Not the ripped orange medallion wallpaper in the first-floor bathroom or the cracked, yellowing linoleum in the kitchen. Not the shabby furniture or the bedspreads on the beds he figured maybe came from the old country several generations ago.

"No," Penelope hurried to say. "Of course not. I'd hate to lose the *Amphitrite.*"

"But I'm out of luck, right? No room at the inn, that kind of thing?" He hoped she couldn't see how much it hurt him to lose his vacation—and to know his old friend had passed away.

"I'm sorry," Penelope said again.

"I can't believe Dan is gone."

"I know," she said softly. "He went much too soon."

She must have loved him very much. It was clear to see Dan's passing still affected her.

Wes forced himself to pull out his cell phone, as much to give him something to do as to find somewhere else to stay. It was nearing dusk, and he needed a roof over his head tonight. Luckily his do-nothing job gave him the funds to handle an emergency. Maybe he could even pick up a few days fishing with some other outfit, if he was lucky. "Got any suggestions where I should stay?"

Penelope looked a little green around the gills herself. "It's the Seahaven Festival this weekend," she said. "Twenty bands spread over two days and nights. It might be hard to find a place in town."

Wes swore. He was sorry for it when Penelope winced, but his luck had run out in a way he wasn't used to. "Forgot all about it. That festival started coinciding with my stay here a few years back. Dan wouldn't give a room to anyone going to it. You had to…"

"Fish to stay with him," Penelope finished for him, laughing a little. "That was Uncle Dan all over. Like I said, I was always on a cruise. I never got to see the festival, and I'm not seeing it this year, either. I'm too busy preparing for the wedding." She considered him a moment, as if trying to calculate what kind of man he was. "I wouldn't normally do this, but I feel awful about letting you down if you've been one of Uncle Dan's regulars. I have a spare room on the top floor. My floor," she explained. "You'd have to share the bathroom with me, and the room is at the back of the house, so no ocean view, but you'd have a roof over your head. I don't know if that helps at all. When the festival is over, there should be some other openings in town."

Wes didn't see how he had any choice in the matter. "That works. I won't be in your way," he promised. "I'll get myself on a boat one way or another… What?" he asked when she pinched her lips together and looked away.

"A lot of the fishing guides pack it in for the weekend when the festival is in town," she explained. "They book festival-goers instead if they have accommodations on land. They can raise their prices to two or three times what they normally get."

"Why didn't you do that?"

"Because I need to break into the wedding scene, and this is the week Olivia wanted to get married. She's going to sing at the festival. According to Amber, she'll 'accidentally' spill it on stage that she's getting married next weekend, and then pretend to be outraged when people use drones or whatever to capture footage of her *private* ceremony."

"What a nightmare," Wes said. "For you, I mean. I'm sure Dan had some pain-in-the-ass guests, but I never saw them."

Penelope made a face. "Believe me, if I could have run charters I would have."

Wes looked at her with new interest.

"Why couldn't you?"

She met his gaze, her dark brown eyes fathomless in the failing light. He saw sorrow in them and a flash of something else—something like pain.

Or was it fear?

"I'll show you to your room," she said. "Do you need a hand with your luggage?"

"I've got it," he said and followed her inside, determined he'd get the answer out of her before the weekend was over.

CHAPTER 2

*W*AS SHE MAKING a mistake?

Electric pricks of nervousness coursed through her as Penelope led Wes into the house and quickly up the central staircase, thankful none of the other guests were in view. She had to be crazy inviting a man to sleep on the same floor as her. Especially a man as handsome as he was. A good five or six inches taller than her, he had the muscular build of a man who pushed himself to be as active as possible. His hair was light brown, his eyes a spectacular blue. A scruff of stubble darkened his strong jaw.

Wes was a man who must be used to women looking at him. Every time she caught his gaze a little thrill coursed through her that had her wanting to shake her head.

The first thing she'd done when she inherited this house was think about how she could configure it so that she'd be safe, no matter who rented the first two floors. She'd installed both a lock and a dead bolt on the door at the top of the stairs. Now here she was about to usher a strange man into her inner sanctum. There were no locks on the bedroom doors within her apartment. She hadn't thought she'd need them.

Send him packing.

Her hand still on the doorknob, Penelope hesitated, her uncle's voice ringing in her mind. Hadn't she learned men couldn't be trusted? Wasn't this exactly why she'd chosen to open a wedding venue instead of running fishing charters? Should she march Wes back down the stairs and out of the house?

No, Penelope decided firmly.

That voice in her head was at odds with the feeling in her gut, which told her that Wes was truly grateful for a place to stay and wouldn't ruin it by trying to make a move on her—no matter how handsome he was. Besides, a man like him wasn't going to fall for someone like her. Every stitch of clothing he wore might be casual, but it was well made. The bag he was carrying with him was designer, if she wasn't mistaken. This rugged stranger had money. He had looks.

He was out of her league.

Besides, she told herself sternly, there were ten other people staying downstairs. If she screamed, she'd have a small army to protect her. Wes had a reservation. He was the last of Uncle Dan's regulars who would ever visit Fisherman's Point.

Coming to a decision, she turned the knob and opened the door.

"Excuse the mess." Penelope had forgotten the hurry she'd been in this morning to make sure the rest of the house was spotless for Olivia's arrival. She hadn't worried about tidying up after herself, since guests didn't belong up here.

They entered into an open area that faced the ocean. Set into the eaves, it wasn't as large as the great room downstairs, but it echoed the feel of it, with a small kitchen, an eating area and a sitting area arrayed in front of large sliding glass doors that led to a generous balcony. Her furniture was second-hand but pretty, the colors bright and sunny.

Unfortunately the sink was full of dishes, a basket overflowed with dirty laundry nearby, the table was piled with paperwork and mail, and several throw pillows were on the floor from when she'd tossed them off the couch the previous evening.

"Looks great to me," Wes said. "I never came to Fisherman's Point for the decor."

Penelope laughed, caught off guard, and then felt guilty since the joke was at her uncle's expense. "I don't think Dan ever even noticed the house," she admitted. "He was all about the fish. There's a bathroom here." She led him down a short hall. "And here's your bedroom." She pointed to the door next to the bathroom. "Mine is at the end."

She couldn't meet his gaze. It hadn't occurred to her how intimate this would feel, or how Wes's broad shoulders and athletic body would seem to fill the small space. He blocked the way back to the living room, and Penelope's thoughts flashed to a different setting over a year ago, when a man had blocked the *Amphitrite*'s companionway, leaving her trapped—

Penelope pushed the image from her mind. She wasn't trapped. Wes wasn't Roger Atlas. Amber, Olivia and eight other members of her entourage were right downstairs and would no doubt come racing up the stairs to complain if she so much as raised her voice.

Besides, Wes didn't look like the type of man who needed to catch a woman unawares if he wanted a good time. He was handsome. Self-assured. Women probably chased him instead of the other way around.

"The room looks perfect," he said as he moved past her into it, still carrying his luggage, unaware of her wayward thoughts. He set down his bags by the dresser and surveyed his surroundings. The walls were pale, but Penelope had done the room up in bright reds and saffron oranges, splashing color around up here since she'd restricted herself to a soothing, neutral palette downstairs. Now she wondered if she'd gone overboard, but Wes seemed happy enough.

She'd forgotten about the pile of boxes she'd left in one corner, some odds and ends she hadn't found a place for yet but wasn't ready to discard, either.

"Sorry," she said again. "I'll get these out of your way."

"You don't have to."

"Yes, I do," she said firmly, grasping the first box and lugging it toward the door. "You're my guest, and you deserve a room that's entirely yours. Just give me one minute."

He stepped back to let her pass before moving to grab another box and follow her. Penelope didn't bother to tell him not to. Men never listened when you said things like that.

She led him into her own bedroom, grateful at least she'd made her bed and wouldn't embarrass herself further. She stored the box by her closet and gestured to Wes to do the same. They repeated the action a second time and then she led him back to his room.

"I'll leave you to settle in. I'm sure you're tired. If you're hungry, feel free to raid the fridge, or I can whip up something for you."

"I'm not hungry, but I'd take a drink if you have one," Wes said. "I'll join you in a minute."

Penelope went to the kitchen, pulled two bottles of beer out of the refrigerator and went out to the deck. It was getting dark. Had she missed Emma and Ava?

No, there they were on their own decks, chatting to each other as the sun dipped under the horizon.

"Hi, Pen," Emma waved and called when she spotted her. "How's your day going?"

"Good. How about you?"

"Same as usual over here."

"Did your guests arrive all right?" Ava asked.

"They did." Penelope moved closer to the side of her balcony. "They're settling in." She couldn't explain much more than that while they were on separate balconies. Anyone could be listening in as they called back and forth.

"Hi!"

Penelope jumped when Wes came up behind her and waved at Emma and Ava, too. "Friends of yours?" he asked her.

"Best friends. That's Ava and that's Emma." She could see their surprise, but there was no way to address that now. "I'll see you two tomorrow," she called to them and led Wes to sit at the little bistro table she had set up at the far end of the balcony. "Did you find everything you needed?"

He picked up the extra beer she'd put out for him. "I did now." He took a sip and studied her. "So, any chance I'm going to get to go fishing?"

"You'll have to look online to see if any of the other guides have an opening after the weekend. Like I said, I have to be on site each day to help prepare for the wedding."

"I'll do that."

She could tell he was disappointed. "You must like fishing a lot."

"I love it. I try to hit somewhere new every year, but I always come back to Fisherman's Point. When I was driving over here from the airport, I was the happiest I've been in months."

And she was letting him down. "Sorry," she said again. "If I'd known you were coming…" She let the sentence trail off. He knew what she meant.

"I'll figure something out."

In the growing darkness, he was close enough she could have reached out and touched him. His fingers were large and blunt, and his shoulders strained the seams of his shirt as he shifted in his chair. She felt that sense of intimacy again. The sense of a man in close quarters. There was something pleasant yet unsettling about the feeling, and Penelope had to stop herself from pushing her chair back to create more space between them. She was going to be around him for several days, at least. Might as well get used to him.

Still, after a long moment, she found herself setting her drink down and standing up. "I'd better make sure my other guests don't need anything. Make yourself at home. I'll be calling it a night when I come back, but you don't have to." It was too early to sleep, but she could watch a movie in her room to pass the time.

"Thanks." Wes's gaze held hers. "For everything. You're going out of your way for me, and I appreciate it."

Uneasy under the frankness of his regard, she hurried inside, where she crossed to the door to the stairs. When she'd shut it behind her again, Penelope stood on the landing, giving her heart time to slow down. She hadn't realized Wes would want to hang out with her as well as sleep in her spare bedroom. It was making her nervous.

Penelope thought it over as she slowly walked down the stairs. Was that really what she was feeling? Was she anxious about Wes?

Or was she attracted to him?

The sound of raised voices on the first level of the house gave her an excuse not to answer that question, and she hurried down to the great room to find Amber and Olivia faced off with each other.

"I don't want to wear that," Olivia cried as Pen approached them. "That color washes me out."

"You'll wear it because you're getting paid twenty thousand dollars to wear it," Amber snapped.

"Hi. Sorry to intrude. I just wanted to see if everything is all right before I call it a night."

"Nothing is all right," Olivia wailed. "I hate both of you and everyone else!"

Amber watched her storm off, then turned on Penelope. "Olivia has been a mess all day because of that incident outside."

"Incident?"

"That man. The one who claimed he had reservations when we booked the whole house. I hope you got rid of him."

"I..." Penelope bit off the words she going to say, realizing that Amber could make all kinds of problems for her.

"When you guaranteed us exclusive use of the house, I understood you to mean full exclusivity," Amber went on. "If you violate that, you've violated the whole contract, as far as I'm concerned."

"Of course," Pen stuttered, thinking Amber herself had already violated it by upping the guest count. "He's long gone." She thought of Wes sitting on her upper balcony. She'd have to get rid of him in the morning. She'd call around to everyone she knew. Surely someone had a couch to spare if nothing else.

"Good. That's one disaster averted," Amber said. "You can go."

Penelope bolted for the stairs, afraid the woman would change her mind and start asking more pointed questions.

"Hold on!"

Pen's heart leaped to her mouth. Had Amber read her mind?

"Under no circumstances are you to enter this space again before ten thirty tomorrow morning. Olivia requires perfect silence until she wakes up."

Pen took this in. "I may need to use the staircase to come down to the front door, but I'll be absolutely silent if I do."

Amber's lips pinched together. "Only the stairs, the front hall and the door. You aren't allowed anywhere else—and no photographs. You are especially not welcome on the second floor, where we all sleep. Are we clear about that?"

"Absolutely." Penelope took the stairs slowly until she was out of Amber's sight, then raced up the rest of them. When she had the door to her apartment locked and bolted behind her again, she went to find Wes.

"Time to come inside," she said softly, locating him on the balcony, still drinking his beer. "It's… curfew," she explained when he looked at her quizzically.

"Curfew?"

"I promised the other party quiet in the evenings," she made up on the fly. Wes nodded. "Look, I'm not sure this is going to work," she added when he'd moved inside, wondering how best to get him to leave after she'd said he could stay. Wes's face fell, and Penelope was unprepared for the corresponding disappointment she felt in her own body. She was intrigued by this man who knew her uncle so well—who knew to ask after the *Amphitrite* by name. She told herself that was all it was, but in truth she was more than intrigued by Wes. She was… interested in him. In every sense of the word. "Tomorrow I'll find you somewhere else to spend your vacation. Until then, I need you to be discreet."

When Wes didn't answer right away, Penelope decided the only thing she could do was come clean. "Look, I promised the other guests the house would be theirs exclusively, and they're not happy about the idea that someone else is staying here, too. In fact…" She shut her eyes, hoping a tell-tale flush wasn't sweeping up her neck. "I told them you'd already left."

"Huh."

Penelope opened her eyes again and waited as Wes considered this. The set of his shoulders was mutinous, and she thought for sure he was going to be angry, but all he said was, "So in other words, I'd better whisper."

"That's right." Penelope wished she could sink into the floorboards. "I really am sorry."

Wes heaved a sigh. "It's okay. I guess I understand."

"You do?"

"I understand that you *owe me one*," he finished and flashed her a quick, conspiratorial grin. "Which means somehow you're going to get me out on your fishing boat before we're done."

Penelope could only gape at him. Was that a threat?

Wes's expression changed in an instant. "Hey, I was joking. I mean, I'd love a chance to see the *Amphitrite* again. It's my favorite fishing boat. I'm not going to strong-arm you into it, though." He smiled again, more tentatively this time, rubbing a hand over the back of his neck. "Kind of hoped you would jump at the chance, if I laid it on thick. Guess I took it too far."

Penelope relaxed again. He was right; normally she would have been thrilled at the chance to take the *Amphitrite* for a spin, but not since the… incident. "I'm scared as hell of Amber and Olivia," she told him. "I'm terrified I'm going to make a mistake, and they'll clear out of here without paying me."

"You need the cash, huh?"

"This is a brand-new business. Without cashflow, I'm toast."

"Believe me, I know," he said ruefully.

"You do?"

He nodded. "Too bad you don't have time to go fishing with me. I don't think I'm going to get the chance to go again for a while and certainly not on the *Amphitrite*."

"It's weird that you know my boat," she told him.

"It's weird that you know *my* boat," he countered. "I mean, the *Amphitrite* isn't mine, but I've got a connection to her. I remember when Dan first got her. He was so proud."

"He was." She'd been proud, too. She'd explored every single nook and cranny of the vessel until the *Amphitrite* felt like her home away from home.

It had been so long since she'd felt the open ocean beneath her. The *Amphitrite*'s wheel in her hands.

Penelope's mind ticked through the possibilities, even though she told herself there was no way she could do anything about that now. Amber didn't want to see her before ten thirty. The *Amphitrite* was fit as a fiddle. And she owed Wes something for kicking him out.

Besides, the thought of being at sea, fishing rod in hand, woke a craving in her she'd been suppressing for months.

And then there was Wes, who was watching her with those unsettling eyes of his. If she took him fishing, she'd get to spend hours with him.

"We leave at four," she told him before she could talk herself out of it. "Four in the morning," she clarified to be sure he understood. "Dress for any kind of weather. It can be changeable out there."

"I've done this before, remember? Four it is." His smile did all kinds of things to her insides.

This time she couldn't help smiling back.

You're going fishing alone with a man? Are you crazy? Her uncle's voice rang in her head.

Maybe, she thought.

But for Wes, she was willing to take that chance.

WES HAD ALWAYS thought of Fisherman's Point as his home away from home, but never before had he felt so comfortable here. Penelope's uncle hadn't spared much thought to the accommodations he offered his guests. Wes, as a favored repeat customer, was usually assigned to one of the larger bedrooms with an ocean view on the second floor of the house, but it had been sparely furnished with ancient bedding. Its walls had been beige, the curtains faded and threadbare.

This room was smaller, and it lacked a view, but it was far cozier. The bedclothes seemed brand-new, the walls freshly painted. The color scheme was vibrant, and the closet and dresser were empty and ready for him, not that he bothered to unpack.

It was a far cry from Dan's hospitality. A far cry from his parents' soulless condo, too. The Abbotts' living quarters were modern and pristine. Their children were banished to the far reaches of the bedroom wing; by the time he was five, he'd been banished from the condo completely. His parents had found him unruly, too loud, too apt to knock over expensive vases and knickknacks. He'd started boarding school in kindergarten and stayed through graduation, with only short visits home on holidays and in summer. Soon after his debut at school, he'd come back to New Jersey to find his old bedroom was now the exercise room. Stuffed with a stationary bicycle, weight machines and an elliptical, his bed had been downgraded to a single set up in one corner. His dresser was gone. So were his toys, packed away for "safekeeping." He lived out of his suitcase and minded his manners, never fully relaxing wherever he was.

Wes nearly groaned at the maudlin turn his thoughts had taken. He was a grown man. He didn't need anyone fussing over him, and whether the walls of his room were beige or a nice warm tone, like these ones, didn't matter a damn bit. Neither did the size or comfort of his bed, although this one looked very comfortable.

He opened his door to find towels and washcloths stacked outside in the hall. The bathroom was small but tidy. When he was done, he came out to find Penelope just exiting his bedroom.

"Brought you an extra blanket," she told him. "It can get cool at night." She was wearing a robe, her luxurious, dark hair spilling down over her shoulders.

Something shifted deep inside him, and Wes swallowed in response to an unexpected surge of attraction for her. It was the jet lag and the overwhelming nature of the day, he told himself. Penelope had created a welcome refuge for him at a particularly trying time. She was young and pretty. Of course he was bound to feel something for her.

He wasn't going to act on it, though. Not when Penelope had taken a chance on welcoming him into her home.

"Thanks," he said. "Good night."

They both shifted sideways to pass each other in the tight confines of the hallway, and Wes escaped into the guest room, shutting the door behind him. He made short work of shucking off his clothes and set his alarm, then played games on his phone for a while before deciding to try to sleep. Once he turned out the lights, however, he found he was wide awake. What a day it had been, one surprise after another, the biggest one being Penelope. He'd been drawn to her the moment he saw her, and it struck him as funny that the celebrity in the house was a drab, petulant teenager and not the warm, curvy, capable woman who'd offered him a room when she could easily have shown him the door.

Why did celebrities these days have to be so troubled? Did they think it made them interesting?

Maybe it did, Wes thought. Maybe audiences liked to focus on other people's problems and forget their own.

He fluffed up the pillows under his head and stared up at the ceiling. He was going to be dead tired at four in the morning if he didn't fall asleep soon, but all he could think about was how short this trip was going to be. Sooner than he wanted to, he'd have to board a plane and see what all the fuss was about in New Jersey—if his parents and Grace didn't patch things up between them.

If perfect Grace couldn't hack running Abbott Enterprises, what hope did he have?

When it became clear he wasn't going to get to sleep any time soon, he pulled out his phone again. He looked up Penelope first. She didn't have a large social media presence, but she featured in a fair number of photographs taken with friends and family. There were shots at the beach, in the redwoods, photos of Fisherman's Point in various stages of renovation. Others showed Penelope clowning around with friends.

He found photos with an older woman who had to be her mother, including a recent series of wedding photos in which that woman was marrying a middle-aged but fit man, surrounded by dozens of family members and friends.

As Wes kept scrolling, he found photos of Penelope with Dan. There they were on the *Amphitrite*, both of them beaming while holding the fish they'd caught. Wes felt another pang at the thought he'd never see Dan again.

In all the photos, Penelope seemed to be single, which shouldn't matter but somehow pleased him. No, he told himself. He was not going to hit on the woman who was giving him a roof over his head.

Still, he found himself absorbing details of her life and wanting to know more.

Next, he looked up Olivia Raquette. She had a much larger presence on the internet, so it wasn't hard to find her. The young diva was ostensibly a singer, but it was quickly apparent she was one of those people who was famous simply because she'd decided to be. She was constantly changing her look, and her fans loved that about her. He found countless photos and videos in which teenage girls copied her latest clothes, hairstyles and dance moves.

None of this was helping him sleep. Wes put his phone on the bedside table and stared at the ceiling for another ten minutes before he sat up in frustration. He'd seen a bookshelf in Penelope's living room. Could he fetch a book without waking her up?

Wes decided to attempt it. He drew on a pair of sweatpants, opened the door carefully and crept down the hall, grateful for the thick carpet that muffled the sound of his steps. In the living room, he breathed a little easier and made his way to the bookshelf he'd spotted earlier. There were books about travel, fishing, the natural world, cooking, embroidery and a large section of historical fiction. He found a mystery novel tucked in among the others and pulled it out.

He had just made it back to the hall when Penelope's door swung open and she nearly collided with him.

Her shriek sounded over-loud in the quiet of the dead of night. Wes caught her as she stumbled, and he dropped his book on his foot in the process.

"Crap."

When he took in Penelope's terrified stare and the way she'd clapped both hands over her mouth, he let go and stepped back. "It's all right. It's just me." She was taking huge gulps of air, her shoulders rising and falling with her breaths. Wes was afraid she was about to hyperventilate. "Penelope, it's me. Wes. You're safe."

Too late, he remembered he wasn't supposed to be here. Had anyone downstairs heard him? Was that why Penelope was so freaked out?

He tensed and listened, her ragged breathing the only sound. When there were no footsteps on the stairs outside the suite, he relaxed. "No one's coming. It's okay. I'm sorry I scared you."

"I—I—" Penelope couldn't seem to find her words. Wes led her to the kitchen, flicked on a light and fetched a glass of water. He handed it to her and waited until she'd taken a drink.

"Are you okay?" He supposed he couldn't blame her

for being startled, but he was worried by how long it was taking her to recover.

"I d-didn't expect you to be standing outside my bedroom door. What were you doing?"

Wes heard the accusation in her question, quickly went to fetch the book he'd dropped in the hall and showed it to her. "Couldn't sleep. Sorry I woke you."

She shut her eyes for a moment. Opened them and took another sip of water. "I thought…" She trailed off, but Wes could guess what she meant, and his heart sank. She was a woman alone with a strange man sharing her apartment. He'd seen the lock and dead bolt on the door that led downstairs. Normally that must give her a measure of safety against her male guests.

"I only got up to find something to read. I'd noticed your bookshelf earlier. I won't do that again." He wanted to reassure her, but he didn't know how.

"It's okay." Penelope's color was returning, and he could tell she was embarrassed. "I overreacted."

"I don't think so. You opened your door in the middle of the night and found me outside it. Of course you were startled."

Thank goodness he'd put something on before traipsing around the apartment. This whole encounter could have been much worse. Penelope wore a pair of soft pajamas, and her hair hung loose below her shoulders. He'd probably never get to run his fingers through that beautiful hair now, he thought.

Not that he was going to in any case, he told himself sternly. Penelope was going out of her way to accommodate him. She was absolutely off-limits.

Which was too bad.

With difficulty, he suppressed his thoughts before they went further in that direction. He wasn't here for a fling, and he certainly wasn't going to put the moves on the woman who was taking him fishing in the morning.

Wes leaned on the counter, wishing he could figure out a way to normalize things again.

"I guess I'm just jittery tonight," Penelope said. "I haven't taken the boat out since Dan died."

"Do you have all the supplies you need?"

She nodded. "I've been keeping it maintained."

"Should I feel bad that I'm pushing you to go out in the morning?"

"No. I can't wait," she admitted. "I'm a little nervous, though."

"Why?" Even if she was rusty with the boat, he knew what he was doing.

She didn't answer for a long time. "I don't even want to put it into words," she said finally. "I hate the way it's been eating at me."

Wes waited her out. In his experience people talked when you gave them time to get their thoughts in order. People liked to be understood.

"The last time I was out on the *Amphitrite*, things didn't go well. I… disappointed my uncle. He made it clear I wasn't welcome to come back. He said I didn't belong on board anymore."

Wes felt her misery as if it was his own. He couldn't imagine being banished from a boat you loved.

Actually, he could. Giving up the *Loose Cannon*, as poor a fishing vessel as it turned out to be, had felt like losing one of his own limbs. He'd put heart and soul into opening his charter business. Losing it so quickly had crushed him.

"Have you ever taken the boat out without your uncle on board?" he asked, wondering what she'd done to anger Dan. Was she careless on board? Was he taking a chance going out with her in the morning? Usually Dan was easygoing, but he didn't suffer fools gladly.

"No," she said simply. "You've nailed it. I've captained her a hundred times. I know that boat backward and forward. But Uncle Dan was always present while I had the helm, and knowing he was angry at me when he died… it's messing with my head."

"I can imagine. You won't be alone out there, though. I've fished for years. I'm capable of helming the *Amphitrite* if anything goes wrong."

After a long moment, she nodded. "Good to know." But Wes could feel she'd withdrawn from him, even though neither of them had moved. What had happened? He searched through their conversation but couldn't figure out where he'd gone wrong.

"I'm looking forward to fishing," he said, wanting to

re-establish the tenuous connection between them.

"We'd better get some sleep then," she said.

Reluctantly, Wes followed her. At his door, he paused.

"Sleep well."

"You, too."

Their brief connection was gone, and Wes missed it. He found himself leaning closer to her before he pulled himself back. What was he about to do? Kiss her? That's all he needed to do after scaring her out of her wits. If he wasn't careful, he'd ruin his chance for a morning's worth of fishing before they'd even started.

He needed to walk away. To go to bed and get some sleep so he could drag his sorry butt back out of it in a few short hours. Instead he heard himself ask, "How old were you when you first started fishing?"

HAD WES ALMOST kissed her?

Penelope's heart beat fast, and her throat was tight with surprise. She was sure he'd leaned in with the intention of doing so before he thought better of it, but why? Hadn't he just assured her she was safe with him? Had he been standing outside her door after all instead of fetching a book like he claimed?

He seemed to be trying to make himself seem as unassuming as possible now, leaning casually against the frame of his bedroom door, one hand jammed deep in the pocket of his sweatpants, the other holding the mystery novel he'd taken from her shelf.

He hadn't kissed her, she reminded herself. He had been carrying the book when they met up. He wasn't trying anything. He'd simply asked a question, and she hadn't answered it yet.

"I've been fishing since I could walk," she said. "Uncle Dan was my mother's brother. He and my dad were friends initially. After several years my dad asked my mom out, with Dan's blessing, and later they were married. When I was little, we'd all go out on Dan's fishing boat together. My mom could fish with the best of them, but she wasn't as excited about it as Dad and Uncle Dan were, so as I got older and didn't need to be watched constantly, she stayed home, and I was the only girl on board. Dad and Dan treated me like one of the crew. I loved everything about it. Unfortunately, my dad died when I was eleven. Taking me out and teaching me what he knew was Uncle Dan's way of honoring my father's memory. There was nothing I liked more than spending every weekend on the *Amphitrite*."

"I can understand that," Wes said. He studied her. "Did that change when you got older?"

"Not really. We went through a bit of a rough spot when I went through puberty. Uncle Dan started calling me a young lady. I hated that. I thought of myself as a deckhand." She laughed, but the memory still hurt. "For a while he tiptoed around me as if I was suddenly breakable. It made me work even harder to prove him wrong." She crossed her arms, hugging herself although she wasn't cold. "He mostly got over it, and we worked together for years until—" She broke off. "Anyway, then last year he died."

She had the feeling Wes knew there was a lot she wasn't telling him.

"I'm sure you're a terrific fishing guide," he said.

"I am. I don't need you or anyone else to tell me that." She immediately wished she hadn't been so sharp. Wes was agreeing with her. She didn't have anything to prove to him.

It was Uncle Dan who'd made her question her abilities—on the boat and off it. Especially when it came to men. If she was afraid of Wes, if she thought him capable of hurting her, she needed to tell him to leave right now.

"You're wishing you hadn't let me stay," Wes said.

Could he read her so easily?

"It isn't that. I'm glad I can honor your reservation. I would have hated to turn you away. It's just... I'm taking a chance letting you sleep up here with me," she said.

"I get that." He frowned. "Kind of sucks that you can't read my mind and see my intentions."

"What would I see if I could?"

"You'd see that I'm a typical man, who's definitely noticed how pretty you are—and how kind," Wes admitted. "And who is also kind of turned on by the fact that you seem to love fishing. But you'd also see I'm a man who was raised right, as far as women are concerned. I'm not going to take advantage of your kindness or the circumstances that are allowing me to sleep on this side of your locked door. I mean that, Penelope. When we're done talking, I'll go back to bed and stay there until you take me out on the *Amphitrite*."

Somehow she believed him. Wes was bigger than her. Stronger, most likely. She didn't feel threatened by him, though. She was very aware of him—as a man. It wasn't fear that had her shivering in her comfy pajamas.

It was his presence. The masculine essence of him that was calling to all that was feminine in her. She was attracted to this man, plain and simple, and it had been a long time since she'd allowed herself to feel that way.

"Okay," she said. "But I'm keeping my eye on you," she added in a mock warning.

Wes smiled. "Glad to hear it. I guess we'd better get some sleep," he added. He didn't move, however, and Penelope had the feeling he wished he could stay. Was Wes lonely like she was? Had he watched his friends pair up and marry while he stayed single? She couldn't imagine a handsome man like him being on his own for very long.

"Good night," she told him before she did something rash, like kiss him herself. Wes pushed off from the wall and watched her walk to her room. When she shut the door behind her and slid under her covers, she was aching with tiredness, but her mind started dishing up visions of the kiss she'd thought Wes had tried to steal. Bad idea, she told herself.

This was a man who'd be in and out of her life in a matter of days. Besides, she needed to focus on making Olivia's wedding an event to remember—

Right after she took Wes fishing.

IN BED, WES thought about the kiss he hadn't stolen from Penelope. He'd definitely wanted to. Luckily some sense of decency had prevailed.

It had been much too long since he'd had a woman in his life. His last girlfriend had been a woman named Heidi, whom he'd met on a fishing trip in southeast Asia. They didn't live on the same continent, so their relationship consisted of shared vacations two or three times a year and a constant stream of jokes, photos and naughty conversations via text. All that had died down this past year, until Wes realized Heidi had moved on.

He hadn't been too upset. In fact, he hadn't noticed she was gone for several weeks, and when he had checked in to make sure he was reading the situation correctly, they were able to have a brief, factual conversation that cleanly ended the affair. Still, it left him at loose ends, and he supposed that was why he was vulnerable to a charged moment like standing in the hall with Penelope in her PJs, wondering what it would be like to draw her close and claim her mouth with his own.

Wes shifted, his body responding to the image he'd

conjured in his head. Although he fought the impulse, telling himself it was dumb to even think of a fling with a woman like Penelope, who seemed the very antithesis of someone looking for that kind of thing, he finally gave in to the fantasy, satisfied himself, got up to deal with the aftermath and tried again to sleep.

He wondered what a woman like Penelope wanted. A committed relationship? Marriage? Did she want children someday, or would she prefer to remain fancy free?

And did she really like weddings enough to angle her entire business around them? Somehow she didn't seem the type.

Wes drifted off on that train of thought and dreamed of fishing boats washing ashore and corporate events in which he was supposed to be the keynote speaker but hadn't prepared a speech.

When he woke to the sound of his alarm, he was so disoriented it took him several long minutes to get his bearings. He shook the remaining shreds of his dreams aside and tossed the covers back. He had a morning's fishing ahead of him, and he intended to enjoy every last minute of it.

He met up with Penelope in the kitchen, where she'd turned on a single light. There were dark circles under her eyes, and Wes felt a pang about how late he'd kept her up and how early she'd risen to make his vacation a good one. She was packing a small ice chest with drinks and snacks.

"Morning," he whispered, mindful of her other guests.

"Morning." She closed the refrigerator and surveyed him. "Good, you're wearing layers. It'll be cool out there, but hopefully it will warm up. Ready?"

"Ready," he confirmed, biting back the retort on his tongue. He was an old hand at this and knew how to dress for a morning on the ocean. Penelope had probably dealt with enough people who didn't over the years, he reminded himself. She was being a good guide.

"We have to be really quiet when we go downstairs. Olivia and her retinue are on the second floor, so going in and out of the main door shouldn't wake them, but it's important that we don't take any chances, okay?"

"Got it." He could be quiet. He took the bags she indicated and followed her out of the apartment and down the central staircase. They made it outside without incident, locked the door behind them, loaded Penelope's CRV and headed out. Once away from the house, Penelope brightened.

"If we woke Olivia there'd be hell to pay," she told him. "Now we can relax. We have to be back by nine thirty, though. She'll up by ten thirty, and I want to look like I've been there the whole time. If Amber guesses I've been fishing with someone else, she's going to feel that she's not getting that one hundred percent exclusivity she wants."

"No problem," he assured her. "I'm just grateful to get any time on the water at all."

He was grateful for the chance to spend more time with Penelope, too. As he'd gotten ready this morning, he was reminded all over again how much care she'd taken to make him feel welcome, despite her obvious concern about having a stranger stay in her personal quarters. She had to be exhausted, but here she was making sure he'd get the chance to fish.

When they reached the harbor, Penelope led him to where the *Amphitrite* was moored. Wes felt a warm glow that the early-morning chill couldn't penetrate. Fisherman's Point might be EdgeCliff Manor now, but the *Amphitrite* was the same as ever, and it warmed his soul to return to her. He patted her gunwale, the feel of the wood beneath his hand a reminder of the happy times he'd had fishing these waters.

A heavily built, deep-sea charter boat, the *Amphitrite* was the finest vessel Wes had ever had the privilege of fishing on. Though its high-end yacht finishes and comfortable furnishings might give the impression that it was nothing but a pleasure craft, Wes knew the *Amphitrite* had been built for function first. Powerful and well-equipped enough to satisfy the most demanding fisherman, the *Amphitrite* could withstand whatever the ocean threw at it.

Wes felt all his cares fading away as they approached the boat.

This was exactly where he wanted to be.

CHAPTER 3

*P*ENELOPE HAD FEARED she'd drag all morning, given how little sleep she'd gotten last night, but the truth was most mornings she rose before the sun, and the fresh air and bracing smell of the sea cleared the remainder of the cobwebs from her mind. At the harbor, she took a moment to text Emma and Ava that she wouldn't be around for their traditional sunrise walk before leading the way to the *Amphitrite*, stepping over the gunwale onto the deck and inviting Wes aboard. She noticed the way he paused and patted the gunwale before he followed her onto the boat and recognized Wes's satisfaction at returning to a vessel he knew well.

The sway of the boat under her feet energized Penelope. She gestured Wes to a seat and began a tour of inspection of the vessel. She'd left it shipshape the last time she'd been on board, of course, but it never hurt to look things over again before departing.

"What can I do to help?"

Penelope found Wes still standing, his hands on his hips, ready to take orders, which disconcerted her. She was used to taking plenty of orders herself from her uncle, but there'd never been anyone for her to boss around, unless it was a client, and you had to handle them with kid gloves.

"I'll have us underway in no time," she told him. "Relax."

"I didn't come here to relax," he countered. "I told you I was studying to be a guide, right?"

"No." He'd never mentioned that.

"I've been fishing all my life. I know my way around a boat, believe me. I'm up for anything you can throw at me."

"Why don't you stow our things and make sure everything is where it ought to be down below?" Penelope said weakly. Her checklist was all in her head. It wasn't like she could hand him a clipboard or something.

"Sure thing." Wes looked amused as he went into the cabin, and Penelope wondered if this was all a big mistake. She should have taken a test run on the *Amphitrite* months ago—alone. She'd been momentarily distracted by her excitement at returning to the sea, but now all her doubts flooded back. Was she making a mistake venturing out alone with a stranger? Was Uncle Daniel right when he'd said she didn't belong on board?

Penelope shook off those traitorous thoughts. Of course she belonged on the *Amphitrite*. She'd taken the helm plenty of times in the past. Uncle Dan had no right to feel superior to her when she was the one who'd kept his business running after his accident had slowed him down. She'd picked up the slack when his drinking had increased, too. She was a capable woman. A capable guide.

So was Wes, apparently, but Penelope wasn't sure how to handle that. Even the most experienced fishermen had deferred to Uncle Dan. Would Wes defer to her?

Or would he try to take over?

Penelope hurried to complete her inspection of the boat. By the time he was on deck again, she was ready to go. As long as she was the one in the driver's seat, so to speak, he had to defer to her.

Didn't he?

She told herself to stop thinking about anything except the job at hand. She needed to keep her mind on the *Amphitrite* and the conditions of the elements around her. Time enough to worry about Wes—and Uncle Daniel—later.

Wes took the seat she'd offered him earlier and remained quiet while Penelope got the boat running.

"Want to help cast off?" she asked him. Uncle Dan often asked clients to do that.

"Sure." He was up again with alacrity, out on the dock, freeing the lines from the cleats that held them in place, jumping back aboard before the vessel strayed too far.

"Thanks," Penelope said. Maybe she could handle

Wes's presence, after all. No part of his behavior had seemed improper since they'd set out this morning, and there was no reason not to take his explanation of why he'd been in the hall outside her door last night as anything less than true. He'd been carrying a book back to his room, after all, when she'd knocked it out of his hands with her door.

Wes wasn't a monster. He was just a regular guy.

That's bad enough, her uncle Dan would say.

Penelope sighed, pushed the unruly tangle of thoughts from her mind and focused on backing the *Amphitrite* away from its slip. She steered the vessel toward the open sea. As they left the marina behind, she breathed a sigh of relief. No major screw-ups so far... not that she made mistakes often, she reminded herself.

"We won't go far," she said, for her own benefit as much as Wes's, raising her voice over the din of the engine. "We don't want to waste too much time getting there and back when we're so limited overall."

"Wherever you want to go," Wes said. "I'm just happy to be on the water."

He was grinning, Penelope realized, and despite her worries, her spirits lifted, too. This was a man who'd already caught the fishing bug and who'd appreciate this day's excursion as much as she did. He'd admitted last night he knew his presence was making her uneasy and had expressed regret that it was so.

She needed to treat Wes like any other charter customer. She could pretend Uncle Dan was snoozing on one of the bench seats at the back of the boat, like he'd done in years past when he'd had too much to drink the night before. There was nothing new or difficult here.

It took forty-five minutes to reach a bay where Penelope knew there'd be fish to catch. She was happy Wes didn't complain about the need to catch some bait fish first. He got to work with a light rod just like she did, and soon enough there were anchovies swimming in the bait well.

"Ready to get serious?" she asked him.

"I've been ready for days," he told her. Penelope felt a pang of sympathy for this man who was obviously built to be out on the water.

"You said you're studying to be a guide. What is it you do now?" she asked as they selected their new rods—large ones that could handle the weight of a lingcod or striped bass.

"VP of Sales," he said.

"What company?"

"Abbott Enterprises."

"Which does....?"

"We're in telecommunications. I won't get into it. We help companies who help companies who help other companies with their connectivity issues."

"Sounds complicated."

"It is."

"Did you always feel a calling to help people with

their connectivity issues?" she quipped, hoping to coax a smile from Wes, who suddenly looked like they were on their way to a funeral rather than a wonderful morning on the Pacific Ocean.

"No. Well, yes and no," he corrected himself. "I like connecting with people, but I can't say telecommunications sets me on fire."

"Why do it, then?"

"Did I mention it was a family business?" He looked past her to the sea and the sky. "It used to be a sweet deal, actually. Few responsibilities. Lots of time to fish."

"Sounds like you'll be fishing all the time soon," she pointed out.

"I hope so."

He didn't sound too sure about that. "Is something standing in your way?"

He nodded, his mouth set in a grim line. "My folks are mad at my sister—so mad they want to give me her job." He must have seen her confusion. "She's the business maven. She's been practically running Abbott Enterprises for years, now."

"So why do they want you to take over?"

"I don't know. She did something they didn't like."

She sensed his growing tension and decided to let the conversation drop. After all, the man was here on vacation. He didn't want to rehash his family dramas.

Penelope moved them near an area where she knew lingcod loved to hide. When Wes baited her rod as well as his, she nearly brushed him out of the way, but she caught herself. He was having fun, and there was no sense angering a paying customer. It was hard not to hear Uncle Dan's voice in her ear, though. *You shouldn't even be out here with him!*

"Everything okay?" Wes asked her.

What had he seen in her face?

"It's fine." She tried not to sound too clipped. Uncle Daniel was gone. She had to make her own decisions now.

As soon as she'd cast her line, she felt her equilibrium returning. She hoped Wes felt similarly. She'd always found that problems that loomed large on land diminished on the water. There was enough space out here to contain them. You could take a mental step back and see the conundrum from all sides. Sometimes new solutions popped up. Sometimes you just gained enough fortitude to muscle through a difficult situation.

"How'd you get into weddings?" Wes asked a few minutes later as their boat drifted slowly.

"I needed to distinguish my vacation rental from all the others in Seahaven," Penelope told him. "When I inherited Fisherman's Point and it was clear I couldn't take over Dan's business, I needed a new way to make the house profitable. I could have made it a straight-up vacation rental, like my friend Ava's, but there are so many of those already in town. I thought about doing a bed-and-breakfast, like my other friend, Emma, did with hers, but again—how would I make mine different from everyone else's? I decided to focus on small, boutique weddings. I figured I could make EdgeCliff Manor into kind of a destination. I based all my decisions on that when I renovated the house."

"You did those renovations?"

"I did."

"They look great. If you ever need a second career, you could go into interior design—or contracting."

Penelope found herself beaming at him. "It was hard with my limited budget," she confessed. "I scoured the area for deals and then tried to make everything go together." Then she'd blown the rest of her money buying furniture and decor Amber planned to pack into a storage container.

"You did a terrific job."

Penelope decided she liked Wes. A tug on her line grabbed her attention. "Oh—got something!"

"Take it slowly," Wes told her, moving closer.

"Seriously? Do you think I don't know how to fish?" Penelope shut her mouth with a snap. Wes was a customer. Let him think he was better at this than she was. What was wrong with that?

"Sorry." Wes stepped back. "I keep forgetting that you're the guide today, not me."

"Have you ever actually run a trip?" She told herself it was her uncle she should be angry at, not Wes, for making her feel so defensive. After all, Wes wanted to be a fishing guide, too. He was probably used to handing out advice.

"A few times. Not as often as I'd like," he admitted.

She bet no one had ever told Wes he didn't belong on a boat.

"Uncle Dan probably wished he could leave Fisherman's Point to you." Penelope kept reeling in her line slowly. The trick with lingcod was to let them get a good hold of the bait fish. Sometimes they didn't get hooked at all; they just held on to their prey until you drew them in close enough to net them.

They didn't speak again until Penelope had landed the fish, an ugly monster of a thing that writhed on the deck until she popped it in the well.

When she'd cast her line again and settled in, Wes spoke up. "What do you mean Dan would want to leave Fisherman's Point to me?"

Penelope wished she hadn't said anything. "He didn't think I had what it takes to be a guide," she said shortly. At least not in the end. Until the incident with Roger Atlas, she'd have said Dan was grooming her to take over his business. "He banned me from the *Amphitrite*."

Wes whistled. "That's rough." He thought about it a moment, then sent a curious glance her way. "What do you think? Do you have what it takes to be a guide? Dan isn't around anymore, after all."

Penelope squirmed under his gaze. "I think I'm a great fisherman."

"That doesn't really answer the question." To Penelope's relief, his attention shifted to his rod.

"Got a bite?"

He nodded, and they repeated the process they'd gone through until Wes landed another lingcod on board. "This is a good spot."

"One of my favorites. One of my many favorites." Pleased with their catch so far, she grinned. Wes grinned back at her. To her relief, he didn't bring up her uncle or guiding again, and he didn't try to take over the *Amphitrite*, either. Instead, they swapped fish stories for the rest of the morning, until Penelope checked the time. "We'd better get back."

"That's got to be the saddest sentence in the English language." He seemed satisfied, though, and Penelope was pleased as she turned the *Amphitrite* for home.

PENELOPE WAS THE guide, he was the client, Wes reminded himself for the tenth time. It didn't matter that he was just as experienced a fisherman or that Dan had doubted her competence for some reason. The *Amphitrite* was Penelope's boat. These waters were Penelope's home turf. So far, she'd proven herself completely competent and gone out of her way to bring him out this morning when she could have turned him down.

This was her rodeo, so to speak. He needed to let her call the shots.

Easy enough to say and a lot harder to do, he

thought when they were setting things to rights before heading home. Several times he'd itched to take Penelope's rod into his own hands to land a fish she was more than capable of landing herself. Now he was itching to take the helm, wanting to feel the heft and sway of the boat under his command as it crested the rolling waves. Every time he thought about his dad's phone calls, he felt like his opportunity to start his own business might be slipping away. He simply couldn't be CEO of Abbott Enterprises, though. This was the life for him. Wide open sky, the heaving of the waves, the tension of a fishing rod in hand…

He didn't ask for a turn at the helm, however, and Penelope didn't offer it to him. Her boat, he reminded himself. Her first time out on the water in months.

He thought about what she'd said, that Dan would have preferred to leave Fisherman's Point and the *Amphitrite* to someone like him. He wished he had an uncle who felt that way. Anything rather than be saddled with the business of guiding Abbott Enterprises into the future. Just thinking about his father's frantic phone calls made his stomach knot.

"What do you do on land for fun around here?" he asked, as if he'd never been in Seahaven before. Usually when he was here he had little time for more than a meal out or maybe a drink at a local watering hole.

"You can visit the redwoods, go surfing, the Pelican's Nest is great for dancing…"

"Maybe we could go sometime." Wes cursed himself the minute the words were out of his mouth. There he went again, hitting on Penelope when she'd made it clear she wasn't interested in that kind of thing.

Her eyes widened and she turned away. "It's going to be a pretty hectic week for me," she told him, busying her hands with a task that didn't really need doing. "Olivia's handler, Amber, is high-strung, and I have to get this wedding exactly perfect. If she trashes me in her reviews, I'm toast."

"Let me know if there's anything I can do to help." He wished he could go back in time two minutes and say anything other than what he'd said. He'd ruined the camaraderie they'd forged this morning. Penelope's shoulders were tense, and she was refusing to look at him.

"Sure."

She was letting him know beyond a shadow of a doubt she wasn't to be flirted with and certainly not to be approached.

Which was too bad. He'd have liked to flirt with her, if he was being honest. He'd told himself he didn't need any entanglements right now, but his short time with Penelope had changed his mind.

"Look, I get that you're really busy, and I understand you don't know me at all, but it sounds like I'm going home in nine days to a real mess." If he even lasted here that long. His father had made no bones about wanting him home sooner. "I don't want to make you uncomfortable. I just want to feel like a human being for a few days. Is there any chance we could see those redwoods or go surfing or hear some live music while I'm here—together? I promise I'll be a gentleman." He held his breath. Would she understand he was being honest?

Penelope gave him a sideways glance.

"Maybe," she conceded. "I have to put this wedding first, but I promise I'll help you have some fun if I can."

Wes let go of the breath he was holding. That had gone better than he'd had any right to expect. "That's all I can ask for."

"I'll start by asking my friends if their husbands will take you surfing while I work today," she added.

Wes bit back the first words that came to his mind: I want *you* to take me. He wasn't a child, and she had a business to run.

"I'd appreciate that." Maybe her friends' husbands could give him the scoop on Penelope.

She started up the boat's engine. Wes settled in to enjoy the ride since he couldn't take the wheel. When they reached the marina, he made sure to wait for her orders and jumped to carry them out as she skillfully docked the boat. He needed Penelope to trust him if he was going to find out what made her tick. And somehow he wanted to figure her out.

His gut kept telling him this might be his last chance at happiness for some time to come, given the crisis waiting for him in New Jersey.

He already hated the thought of leaving the Pacific Ocean, the *Amphitrite*—and Penelope—behind.

"WE'RE LATE," PENELOPE said, slipping her phone into her pocket and eyeing the sun, which was now well over the horizon. "I should have turned us back a lot sooner."

"I wasn't watching the time. Next time we'll have to set an alarm," Wes said, as if he was somehow responsible—and as if they were going to do this again. She supposed he was responsible in a way; she wouldn't have been out on the water if he hadn't requested a trip. Now she felt silly she hadn't taken the *Amphitrite* out before. Why had she waited until she was besieged by guests to enjoy it?

She felt bad now that she'd given Wes a hard time about helping. Maybe if she hadn't been so stubborn, they would have gotten back sooner. She pulled out her phone again and calculated the time it would take to stow things away, deal with the fish and put the *Amphitrite* to bed until the next time they went out.

"I can take care of things here," Wes said. "I know you don't trust me yet, but I know my way around a fishing boat—and around fish. You take the car. I'll get things ship-shape around here, gut the fish and call for a ride."

"You can't take a bucket of fish in a ride share."

"Sure I can. In a pinch, I'll walk back," he said over

her protestations. "It's not far."

"But—"

"Penelope, I won't let you down. I swear."

Could she trust him? Should she? Somehow it seemed like a betrayal to the *Amphitrite* to hand her over to a near stranger.

"You're going to be late," he said.

"Fine." She handed him the keys. "But be careful. This boat is important."

"All boats are important, but you're right, the *Amphitrite* is special." Wes was already turning to get to work. "I'll snap some photos to show you when I get back so you can see what I did."

She nodded unhappily and hurried to her car. She could just make it home in time if traffic went her way. Starting the engine, she waited impatiently until a large truck edged its way past her through the crowded parking lot and then she pulled out, turned and floored the gas until she reached Cliff Street. There was no way to speed here when it was tourist season; she dawdled along behind a Camaro driven by a redhead in a pink-polka-dotted beach cover-up. By the time she pulled into the parking area behind Fisherman's Point—EdgeCliff Manor!—Penelope's heart was beating double-time.

She slipped the key in the front door's lock carefully and opened it just enough to slip inside. She held her breath as she darted up the two flights of stairs to her apartment, dashed into the shower, rinsed off as quickly as she could, did her hair in two fat braids wound around her head and slipped on a wrap dress she'd laid out for herself earlier.

As she came downstairs again at exactly ten thirty, she bumped into Amber on the second story landing.

"I haven't woken Olivia up. You're early!" Amber hissed.

Penelope pulled out her phone and held it up as the clock changed to 10:31. "You're late," she countered and kept going.

Downstairs she found Olivia's entourage in strength, tiptoeing around with exaggerated care. A young woman—Chelsea—handed her a cup of coffee. A man wiped the counter as soon as Penelope pushed away from it. Had she left a handprint? Penelope stopped herself from rolling her eyes.

"Let's get to work," Amber said, striding into the room. "Olivia will be down momentarily."

"Can't wait," Penelope said.

"…DON'T FIX IT, I'm leaving," someone was shrieking as Wes opened the door to Fisherman's Point—EdgeCliff Manor, he corrected himself with an inward groan. Penelope had been right; the driver of the rideshare car he'd called refused to transport a cooler full of freshly caught fish, and Wes had ended up hoofing it home. The walk had been somewhat longer than he'd expected, made awkward by the bulk of his cooler and the throngs of tourists on the sidewalk. He'd seen a squad car cruise by slowly, the policeman driving it checking him out, and he wondered if he looked worse for wear for having spent the morning on the ocean.

"We discussed this before," another female voice said. "This is the color the sponsors picked."

"I don't care about the sponsors. I don't care about any of this. You need to fix this, now!"

"It really is a pretty color," a softer voice said.

That was Penelope, Wes thought. The woman shrieking was Olivia, and Amber was the one trying to dictate terms—and failing.

Sure enough, Olivia rounded the corner into the hall at high speed but stopped when she caught sight of Wes and his giant cooler.

"What's that?"

"Fish."

"Fish?" Olivia's nose wrinkled up. "Dead fish? You brought dead fish into the house where I'm going to get married?" Her voice slid up the scale, taking on more volume as it went. Amber popped around the corner, too, her eyes widening at the sight of him.

"What are you doing here?" She turned on Penelope, who'd followed her. "What is he doing here—in our house? You said we had exclusive access to it. You said there'd be no other guests."

Hell. He'd forgotten that promise. He was blowing things for Penelope, big time.

"I'm not staying here," he lied. "I'm just delivering the fish. For the party."

"Party?" Amber said. "What party?"

Double hell. He'd figured a singer would have parties all the time.

"The... after-party," he scrambled to say. Didn't bands always have after-parties? That festival started today. Wasn't she performing at it? Surely she'd have people over afterward.

Olivia brightened and turned to Amber. "Are we throwing a party tonight?"

"The day before you perform? Of course not," Amber said. "Besides, no one can see this place until your wedding!"

"I guess you won't need fish, then," Wes said.

"I ordered them for my friend, Emma," Penelope said quickly. "She owns the bed-and-breakfast two doors down and had an emergency this morning. It's her party the fish are for. I'll get those to her right away," she said to Wes, giving him a sharp look as if to warn him to go along with the story.

"I'll... be going then," he said, not sure what else to do. He'd have to sneak back in later—but how?

"I thought you were a guest," Amber said. "Didn't you say you had a reservation yesterday?"

"That was all a big misunderstanding," Wes said. He thought quickly, trying to come up with a plausible story. "I'm new in town. Came to work on a fishing boat.

My… apartment isn't available yet so I booked a couple of nights in a vacation rental."

"The one next door," Penelope supplied. That would work as cover if Amber noticed him hanging around again.

"Boring!" Olivia exclaimed. She held up a slinky bit of fabric he supposed might be a dress. "Do you really think it's pretty?" she asked Penelope.

"It's… gorgeous?" Penelope said uncertainly.

Olivia's face fell. Wes came to the rescue again.

"I think they're fabulous," he told Olivia. "Your sponsors have wonderful taste. Are you sure you didn't give them a hint about what you wanted?"

Olivia blinked. "A hint?"

The color of the fabric reminded Wes of the setting sun he'd watched slipping below the horizon of the ocean last night. Olivia's social media feed was full of sunsets like that—with her in the foreground, of course.

"Sunsets are kind of your brand, right? Like when you were photographed with Alfonso on the French Riviera?" He named a major fashion mogul he'd seen in her feed. "And when you were having cocktails with the Bad Marias in Cabo?" Olivia had been front and center in that photo even though the Bad Marias were a much more popular music act than she'd ever been. "Don't you think the color of that outfit will evoke your brand?"

Olivia perked up. "You're a fan?"

"Of course I am. It's great to meet you in person, by

the way."

Olivia fairly glowed. "I'm always happy to meet a fan. You're right. Sunsets are part of my brand. Okay, I approve," she told Amber. "I don't know what you're making such a fuss about."

"Oh, you know me." Amber's face betrayed none of her emotions. Wes figured keeping them tightly controlled was crucial to her job. "Olivia needs to eat now," she announced. "Everyone out, but stay close," she said to Penelope. "We have a lot of work to do today."

"Of course." Penelope turned for the stairs. Wes followed her, then remembered he wasn't supposed to be staying here. Penelope must have remembered, too. "Can you carry the cooler upstairs for me?" she asked him. "I'll meet up with Emma later, and I have a few things to discuss with you."

Amber narrowed her eyes. "What do you need to discuss with him?"

"Mr. Abbott is helping me with arrangements for future guests. This way, Mr. Abbott."

"Coming," Wes said.

They hurried up the stairs before Amber could protest. When they were safe in the third-floor apartment, Penelope turned to him. "That was close. I don't think Amber bought our explanation. There's going to be hell to pay later."

"Why don't you pretend to hire me as an assistant?

That would give me a reason to be here late—and early, for that matter. If they notice me here at odd hours, I could say I was working for you. Amber and Olivia can't object to that."

That wasn't exactly true. Wes figured they could—and would—object, but he didn't want to leave. He liked the comfortable little room down the hall from Penelope and hoped he could convince her to take out the *Amphitrite* again.

"You just told them you're working on a fishing boat."

"In the mornings," Wes said. "I have my afternoons free, as it turns out. Tell them you needed some extra help and hired me for the rest of the day."

She looked like she'd argue with that but in the end said, "I guess I can do that, but it means you'll have to look like you're working."

"I will work—if you take me out fishing again to-morrow."

Penelope rolled her eyes. "Fine," she said, drawing out the word in a growl. "We'll go out again tomorrow, but that's the last time. All right?"

"If you say so."

"Your first assignment is to get out of my way. I need to freshen up and get back down there before there's a mutiny."

Wes retreated to his room and waited until he heard the door close and Penelope's tread on the stairs down to the lower levels of the house before he emerged again. He figured with all the fuss she'd forgotten to contact her friends about surfing, so he decided he'd entertain himself. He quickly showered and headed out for a walk and to grab lunch at his favorite Seahaven restaurant, Spice Time.

He kept himself busy at the beach the rest of the day, and ate dinner out as well, but came straight home to EdgeCliff Manor afterward, hoping to get some time with Penelope on the deck. Careful that no one saw him slip inside and dart up the stairs, he spotted her standing by the sliding glass doors when he let himself into her apartment, her back to him, her phone pressed to her ear.

"Amber was so happy Wes convinced Olivia to wear the dress her sponsors gave her, she stopped questioning why he was here, thank goodness," she was saying into it. "Olivia is so picky about everything, and Amber is ready to attack at the slightest provocation. I have no idea how I'm going to get through this." She listened for a minute. "Thanks for offering. I'll take you up on it if I think of something, but I don't know how you can help." Another pause. "Wes? He's... nice." She listened a beat. "Okay, he's hot, too, but mostly nice. You know I'm not going to do anything with a guest."

Wes was happy to hear she found him attractive but less so to find out she had rules about fraternizing with guests. He'd promised himself he wouldn't try anything with her, but it had been fun to consider what could happen between them.

"This morning?" Penelope went on. "I took him out on the *Amphitrite*. We went fishing." A pause. "I know, right? Took me long enough. Wes is a fishing guide. He could help me if anything went wrong." Penelope suddenly let out a frustrated groan that made Wes jump. He hadn't expected it, and he was half moving to rush to her aid when she threw her free hand in the air. "Why do I keep doing that? Why do I keep undercutting my own capabilities? The *Amphitrite* is mine. Uncle Dan isn't around anymore." She listened for a minute. "Wes? He was fine on the boat. I'm sure he's very competent, too, but I don't want anyone's help. I want my own self-confidence back, and I'll tell you what. Hosting Olivia Raquette's wedding isn't doing a damn thing for it."

Wes told himself there'd be no hanging out on the deck tonight. Penelope was stressed out, and he was part of the reason. He'd pushed her to take him fishing this morning, and his presence had made Olivia and Amber upset. He wanted his fishing trip, but he didn't want to ruin Penelope's business. From now on he'd be the perfect guest, he told himself, and slipped off to his room without her even knowing he was there.

CHAPTER 4

*W*ERE THERE ANY waters in which Wes hadn't fished? So far on their morning's excursion he'd told her about catching marlin in Australia, trout in the Orkney Islands and swordfish in Sicily, all dream experiences for most normal fishermen. Meanwhile, she'd never fished anywhere but California. Penelope felt positively provincial in comparison. At least she'd gotten some sleep last night. Wes had slipped in and gone straight to bed while she'd been talking to Ava. Unexpectedly, she'd been disappointed he hadn't joined her on the deck to wind down and she'd gone to bed early, too, where she'd slipped straight into a dreamless sleep. The next time she opened her eyes, her alarm was going off.

Wes was now regaling her with a tale of his battle with a hundred-pound roosterfish in Cabo San Lucas. "They're not the biggest fish, but they fight harder than anything else I've encountered," he was saying. "It struggled for hours, and that was after I'd waited most of the day for one to appear. They're elusive, and they'll crush your baitfish and disappear in a flash if you let your guard down, even for a minute."

"Sounds exciting."

"It was, but it was hot, too, and the boat had barely any shade. I thought I'd pass out from heatstroke before I brought it in. The captain kept trying to take the rod from me. We nearly got into a fight over it, but I refused to give up."

"It would be disappointing not to land it yourself after all that effort."

"Exactly." He grinned at her. "What about you?"

"Me?" She couldn't top the locations where he'd fished, but she could amuse him with stories of some of the characters she and her uncle had guided. "One of the more interesting trips we chartered was a bride and groom from Kentucky who were on their honeymoon. We did a three-day stint up and down the coast. Apparently, the groom arranged the whole thing. He told his bride they were going on a California cruise, and she was quite pleased about the whole thing until they climbed on board and she noticed all the fishing gear. Had to be the most awkward thing I've ever seen."

Wes chuckled. "Did she divorce him?"

"I wouldn't have blamed her if she did, but actually, she rallied pretty quickly and was a really good sport— and a good fisherwoman, too. We kept the booze—and food—flowing, and soon enough she was reeling them in with the best of them. She made her husband swear they'd take a real honeymoon within six months and told him she was never trusting him to book a trip again."

"Glad it worked out," Wes said, casting his line.

"Me, too." She sobered up. "One of the worst trips we ever did was a with a father and two young sons. That was a day for beginner's luck, if there ever was one. Those kids pulled in fish after fish all day long. Meanwhile, Dad couldn't catch a damn thing. He cussed us out. Threw a fishing rod overboard. By the time they left, the kids were miserable. They couldn't enjoy their accomplishments at all because their dad was so jealous of them."

"That sucks." Wes concentrated on his line a second, making an adjustment. "You can never predict how fishing will go."

"You certainly can't," she agreed.

"What's your favorite type of group to host?"

She thought about it. "Families, generally. The kind where they've been going fishing together all their lives. Grandparents, parents and kids. That's a lot of fun. The worst are the drinking buddies who think they're fishing buddies but start hitting the coolers before the sun is all the way up."

"The rowdy ones?"

"Exactly. Combine sun, water, alcohol and a healthy dose of boredom interlaced with stiff competition, and it can be a toxic mix. Then there are the ones who are jerks all on their own. One time, this guy—" She snapped her mouth shut. What was wrong with her? She didn't need to tell Wes about that. "This guy threw up all over the catch," she amended lamely. It wasn't exactly a lie. That had happened, too. She put all her concentration on her line. They'd had few bites so far. Maybe it was time to move and try somewhere else.

WHAT HAD PENELOPE meant to say before she switched stories? Wes watched her out of the corner of his eye, but she'd busied herself with her fishing line and was making it clear she was done with the conversation. Some guy had done something worse than throw up on the catch, although that was pretty gross if you asked him. Had some boozer gotten belligerent? He'd seen that on a couple of his trips. Some people weren't content with a party until fists were thrown.

He remembered what she'd said about her uncle banning her from the boat. What had she done to deserve that?

He wasn't dumb enough to ask.

He checked the time. "Let's head back," he said, although they could have gotten away with fifteen more minutes of fishing.

"Sounds good." Penelope confirmed his suspicions that she'd be grateful to return to EdgeCliff Manor early enough to be sure to be on time for Olivia and Amber and the rest of their crew.

When they'd made it to the dock, Wes jumped to

help batten down the ship, and they worked together methodically until they were on their way to the house.

"Do you have any errands for me to run?" he asked when they parked in Penelope's spot.

"Errands?"

"I'm working for you, remember?"

"I—can't pay you," she said. "I'm maxing out my credit cards to get through this week."

"You don't need to pay me," he assured her. "You're getting up at four o'clock to get me out on the water despite having a full day's work ahead of you. I appreciate it more than I can say." He wished he could touch her, but that was out of the question, especially after what he'd overheard last night. He needed to be a gentleman. He could enjoy Penelope's companionship on the water without hitting on her. No need to complicate anything.

Even if complicating things sounded pretty good right now. The wind on the ocean had tousled her curls, and her cheeks were bright. He loved the way she was so comfortable on board. There was nothing fussy about Penelope. She didn't shirk hard work or shy away from the smellier parts of the job.

She was fun, he thought. Vibrant.

Sexy.

And that was enough of that, he told himself.

"Well." Penelope thought about it as she got out of the car. "We could use some fresh vegetables. Salad stuff, the kind of things I can use to make a veggie plate."

"I can do that." Wes climbed out, too, and went to join her near the back of the vehicle. He'd have to look up veggie plates as soon as he was out of Penelope's sightline. Make sure he was picturing the right thing.

"Maybe if I ply Olivia with food, she'll be less cranky," Penelope said. "She's so skinny she must be half-starving all the time."

"Just as long as she fits in her wedding dress next week," Wes said.

Alarm flashed over Penelope's face. "You're right. I'd better not feed her too much."

"I'm sure you'll figure out the exact right balance between crudites and calories." Without thinking, Wes bent down to brush a kiss over her cheek, then remembered he had no right to and pulled back so sharply he nearly backed into the CRV. Penelope sucked in a surprised breath, and he wanted to kick himself. How had he forgotten his own rules so quickly? "Sorry. Habit. I feel like we've been friends forever." He braced himself, expecting her to tell him off.

"You barely know me," she said. Pink suffused her cheeks, and he had the feeling she was calculating how quickly she could get from the car to her door.

"But I want to know you," he told her truthfully. "I'm attracted to you. What's more, I like you. I want you to feel comfortable when we're out on the *Amphitri-*

te, though, and now I've probably screwed it all up."

"You're damn right you've screwed it up. How can I do my job when I'm afraid you're going to accost me every time I turn around?

Accost her? Ouch. Did that mean she wasn't attracted to him? Once or twice he thought she might be.

"I won't," he promised her. "Hit on you. On the boat." He was being as articulate as a teenager on his first date, but he hoped Penelope could read the truth of what he was saying in his face. He'd never been accused of accosting anyone before, and it pained him to know Penelope could be afraid of him. Or maybe disgusted was a better word.

Either way, he felt like a heel, and it wasn't comfortable. The moment stretched out between them until he didn't think he could stay here another second. He had messed up badly, and he—

"Are you reserving the right to hit on me on land?" Penelope asked.

It took him a minute to realize she had made a joke. A kind of funny one.

Wes hesitated, wondering if this was a trap. "Can I?" he asked unevenly. "Because the truth is, I'd like to."

Penelope laughed. "You're incorrigible, you know that?"

Wes breathed a sigh of relief. So he hadn't ruined everything. "That's what my parents always said." When she didn't answer, he touched her hand. "I really am sorry. I have a lot of female friends who regard a kiss on the cheek as a reasonable goodbye. I could pretend that's all that was, but I won't, because you deserve the truth. I'm interested in you. I'd like to get to know you better. If you don't feel the same way, I'll drop it, and I certainly won't force my attentions on you. I know how to behave."

"That's what you said before, and yet you just made a move," she pointed out.

"I know. Chalk that up to getting carried away. It won't happen again."

"I can't be interested in you. I have too much going on. You saw what I'm dealing with here." She gestured toward the house.

"Then let's just be friends," Wes said, keeping his voice light although the rejection stung. "Really, I mean it. If you want any accosting done, you'll have to do it yourself. I'll stay over here until you tell me otherwise."

She sighed. "I shouldn't believe you. I guess I'm just a sucker." She opened the back of the CRV and fetched out a few things to carry upstairs. "I'll let you get to your errands. Would you mind picking up coffee, too? Cups & Waves is my favorite. I'll take a mocha."

"Sure thing. I'll look up the address." She was handling this with more grace than he was feeling, although she refused to look him in the eye.

"Say hi to Kamirah for me if she's there," Penelope said briskly. "Tell her I'll be in soon to hear how her classes are going. She's one of the baristas."

"Will do."

"And keep your phone on in case I need anything else."

"Sure thing. I won't be long. Penelope?"

"What?"

There were a million things he'd like to say to her. "Thank you—for the best morning I've had in months."

She met his gaze this time, and a rush of wanting filled him, catching Wes off guard. Generally speaking, it wasn't hard for him to find a woman willing to give him a try, but he realized now his prior girlfriends had something in common. They'd never looked at him the way Penelope was looking at him now. He picked women who were self-involved, busy or distant or so tangled up in their jobs or circumstances they had to pencil him in around the edges. He picked women so lovely they were used to being worshipped and didn't feel they needed to return the favor.

Penelope was lovely, too, but in a whole different way, and right now she was here with him, *present* in a way he found disconcerting. She wasn't just looking at him; she was seeing him—

And it was turning him on.

"You're welcome," she said and hesitated before adding, "I'm happy you're here."

Wes found himself swallowing hard as she turned and made her way inside.

People must have said that to him before a thousand times, but something about the way Penelope said it was different. She meant it. He didn't know how he knew that. He just did. Her uncle Daniel was a straight shooter. He had the feeling Penelope was, too. Few people around him in his life had been so forthright.

He thought over their conversation as he walked to his rental car and got in. Penelope had said she couldn't afford entanglements, not that she didn't want them. Maybe there was still hope. He wouldn't push his luck, but he'd let her know he was available—if she changed her mind.

He found the address for Cups & Waves, and a quick internet search brought up the name of a small urban farm by the name of Heaven on Earth. Intrigued, Wes made his way across Seahaven to the south side of town and located the small wedge of property. Fronted by a large Victorian house, the lot was cultivated to within an inch of its life as far as he could see. A sign announced that the farm's wares could be bought at a local farmers market on Saturdays and Wednesdays, but there was also a small stand with an honor system box for cash.

Wes picked out a head of broccoli, a cauliflower and other vegetables that could be chopped up and served with dip. On the way home, he bought some fresh bread, artisan cheese and dip at a store. He liked the way everyone was so friendly here in Seahaven. People greeted each other by name often. Neighbors stopped to chat in the aisles of the stores.

Would he ever have a community like that in New Jersey?

Somehow Wes doubted it. He'd never managed it before, and he wouldn't have time if he became Abbott Enterprise's CEO. He'd have to work night and day to learn how to run the company. He'd socialize with people who called him boss, which meant he wouldn't have any true friends. What little time he'd have off would be spent catching up on errands and exercise.

It all sounded hideous.

He stopped at Cups & Waves last and saw immediately why Penelope loved it so much. It was everything you wanted a local coffee shop to be. The young woman behind the counter, her braids wound into an elaborate bun atop her head, sang Penelope's praises as soon as he mentioned her name.

Wes had only been gone an hour, but when he walked through the door into EdgeCliff Manor, it was clear things weren't going well. He set the little tray of coffee cups on the stairs, since he hadn't brought some for everyone, and kept going into the great room.

"It's too small," Olivia was yelling. "It's all so damn small. Why didn't we rent an arena?"

"Because we're going for exclusive and mysterious," Amber told her. "Your brand is overplayed right now. We need to build it up again."

"With the sliding doors open, it is really quite spacious," Penelope said as Wes entered the great room. Both of the women turned on her.

"Spacious?" Amber said in disbelief.

"My bathroom at home is bigger than this," Olivia snorted. "Spacious. What a joke."

"Time for a snack," Wes crowed, barging in between them, remembering what Penelope had said earlier. He juggled his bags of groceries as if he had an armload of them instead of just the two. "I've got fresh bread and local cheese. I'll have them out in a jiffy."

"Olivia doesn't eat carbs or fats," Penelope hissed, grabbing the bags from his hands. She carried them to the kitchen area. "Where are the vegetables I sent you for?"

No wonder Olivia was so quick to anger, Wes thought. No carbs or fats? Just kill him now. Olivia was skinny, with dark circles under her eyes that all the makeup in the world didn't seem to cover, but he'd figured that was her take on heroin chic. Now he wondered if it was simple malnutrition.

"Right here." He came to pull them out of the bags but stepped back when she immediately began to wash and chop them. After a moment's search, he found a cutting board and knife of his own and set up a plate of bread and cheese. When Penelope put a platter of veggies and dip on the counter, he set his creation beside it.

"Now you have a choice. I wasn't sure if you were a

transitionist, Olivia, so I wanted to cover all my bases," he said.

"A transitionist? What's that?" Amber asked suspiciously, eyeing the platter of bread and cheese as if it might do something unexpected.

"Someone who is transitioning from low carb to *balanced* carb. It's a new thing out of Seattle," he explained, although he was making it all up. He knew people who legitimately got ill from eating certain types of grains and hoped Olivia wasn't one of them, but he had a feeling she was at the mercy of every trend that came along. Maybe he could help her start a new one in which she got to feel full for once. "Penelope? I wondered if you had a minute to go over the schedule for this afternoon. I want to be sure I can get everything done."

"Sure," Penelope said slowly. "If you can spare me a minute, Olivia?"

"Yeah," Olivia said ungraciously. "Whatever."

Wes led the way. As they passed the stairs, he grabbed the coffee and brought it outside with them.

"What are we doing?" Penelope asked, taking her cup. "Besides savoring our coffee. Thank you, by the way."

"We're giving those two women a chance to eat," he said. "Kamirah says hi back, by the way. She said classes are going great."

"Awesome." Penelope took a sip of coffee. "What

happened to making sure Olivia fits in her wedding gown?"

"One crisis at a time. She was going to devour you alive if she didn't get something else to eat first."

"I'm pretty sure I can handle her—and Amber."

"Of course, you can," he assured her. "But a little bread and cheese won't hurt."

"I DON'T THINK I can handle any of this," Penelope said when she managed to slip away to Emma's house late that afternoon. Amber had taken Olivia upstairs to prepare for the concert that night, so Penelope thought she could venture out for twenty minutes without being missed. "Olivia hates my guts, and her handler, Amber, isn't much better."

"Maybe she's nervous about tonight," Emma suggested, placing a frosty glass of lemonade decorated with a sprig of mint on the counter in front of Penelope.

"Maybe she's nervous about her wedding, too," Ava added, accepting a glass as well. "That can make anyone grumpy."

"Maybe. Whatever it is, the two of them are driving me up a wall. You know, no one ever pampered me like Olivia gets pampered, and I can still get out of bed in the morning. Meanwhile, Olivia is miserable all the time." She told them about Wes's trick of leaving them alone with the food. "By the time we got back, about a quarter of the vegetables were gone, and the plate of bread and cheese was empty. I have to admit, both of them were more mellow afterward, but they certainly weren't cheerful."

"We missed you on our walk again this morning," Ava said.

"Sorry about that. It's the only time I can take Wes out, and I don't want to disappoint him. He thought he was going to get nine days of fishing with Uncle Dan." She fought the flush of heat rising in her cheeks as she thought about Wes. He'd said he was attracted to her. He liked her.

She'd blown him off.

Now she was regretting it, even as she told herself it was the only sensible thing to do. She was already in over her head with this wedding, and Wes wasn't going to stick around.

"Of course." Ava smiled. "You're only doing it to be a good host."

"That's exactly right." Penelope hoped she was hiding her embarrassment. "I have a good time when I'm fishing with Wes, but that's all that's going on between us." Anything else would be playing with fire.

If only she could meet a man as interesting as Wes who was making his home here in Seahaven. Someone she could get to know over a longer span of time. She hadn't had a date since she'd inherited Fisherman's Point, and she missed having someone special in her life. Emma and Ava were married. They were getting on with things.

What about her?

"Which do you like better? Fishing or running the wedding business?" Ava asked casually.

"Fishing." Penelope stopped herself. "But I've barely given the wedding business a chance. Not everyone will be as demanding as Olivia."

"I think the word *bridezilla* has entered our vocabularies for a reason," Ava countered.

"Ava, hush. Penelope's right," Emma said. "This is her first wedding. It's way too soon to make any judgments about her business. She's worked hard to renovate her home, and she's made a beautiful wedding venue out of it. She's going to rise to the occasion. When Olivia's wedding is over, she'll have the kind of publicity she needs to get more customers. Everything is right on track."

"Sorry," Ava said. "You're totally right, Emma. Penelope has got this. The wedding is going to be wonderful."

"I hope so," Penelope said doubtfully. She appreciated Emma's reminder to Ava about how much effort she'd put into her house, but the way Olivia and Amber kept criticizing everything made her think maybe it was all for nothing. "My twenty minutes are up. I'd better get back."

"Olivia is performing tonight?" Emma asked.

"She's the headliner. I didn't even consider getting

tickets because I was so afraid I'd need to work every moment, but Amber hardly lets me do anything anyways."

"I didn't feel like braving the crowds," Ava said.

"We aren't going, either," Emma said. "Look at us, a bunch of stick-in-the-muds. We need to do better."

"Next time there's a music festival we'll go together," Ava promised. "That would be fun."

"It would," Penelope said. Next time she wouldn't be trying to throw a wedding for the world's most particular bride.

At EdgeCliff Manor Penelope found Amber in consultation on the stairs with several members of Olivia's entourage.

"What's happening?" Penelope asked, wishing she could simply edge around them and see if Wes was in her apartment.

"Preparing an artist for a show is a delicate operation," Amber snapped at her. "Olivia is about to emerge. Step back."

Penelope did so, retreating down a step and pressing her back against the wall. A moment later Olivia's door flung open, and the star herself appeared in the flimsy outfit she'd been so unhappy with before. Penelope wondered what the fuss was about: the dress was so tiny its colors barely mattered. Her makeup was dramatic, done up to be visible from the last row, Penelope assumed. She tottered on a pair of heels so high,

Penelope wasn't sure how her feet bent to accommodate them.

"Formation!" Amber cried.

Olivia's entourage formed two lines on the stairs. Olivia began to walk down between them, each pair holding her elbows and passing her down to the next step. When she reached Penelope's level, Pen realized she'd need to do her part, but before she could grasp Olivia's forearm, Olivia stopped.

"Tickets!" she cried.

One of her assistants jumped, rummaged in her pockets and held out an envelope. Olivia opened it, fanned out a set of tickets and presented them to Penelope. "You'll come to the show, of course."

"Thank you." Penelope was almost too surprised to take them, but she got her wits about her and did so, shoving them into her pocket. She took Olivia's arm and helped her down the next step. As Olivia descended, the rest of the entourage pushed past Penelope to sort themselves into lines again, ready to do it all over again.

Two minutes later the house was empty. Penelope took a deep breath, let it out and turned to slowly climb the rest of the stairs to her apartment. When she finally let herself in, she felt like she'd sprinted a marathon.

"Hey, you're here." Wes stood in her kitchen, setting two cold beers on a platter of cheese, bread, vegetables and dip that looked suspiciously like what they'd fed Olivia and Amber at lunchtime. "Want to sit on the deck?"

"Yes." She remembered the tickets. "Except I guess I have a concert to go to." She explained what had happened.

"Do you want to go to Olivia's concert?"

"Not really." Penelope felt guilty about that, but she'd been up since four in the morning and was exhausted.

"Then let's stay here. I bet you can find someone who'd be thrilled to get them."

It took some calling around, but Kate, Aurora, their employee, Connor, and some of their friends were glad to come and get the tickets. Soon Penelope was able to settle in on the deck.

"OLIVIA AND AMBER didn't eat very many vegetables this morning," Penelope said after they'd contemplated the ocean for some time.

"They demolished the bread and cheese," Wes told her with satisfaction.

"So you're a mind-reader as well as a star-whisperer."

Was that a little tartness in Penelope's tone? Wes wondered how to smooth things over. He'd always been good in a crisis, especially when it came to soothing people's tempers. It was his superpower, which was why his parents required his presence at every corporate gathering.

"I like people. Always have," he said.

"So you're an extrovert."

"Aren't you? You're running a wedding venue. I'd have thought that was a requirement."

Penelope sighed. "Maybe I should have considered that before I started renovating Fisherman's Point."

"EdgeCliff Manor is beautiful," he said softly. "Your skill and handiwork are evident in every corner of it. You should be proud of what you've done here."

"Olivia and Amber hate it." She shut her eyes, leaned back in her chair and sighed again.

Wes didn't like the sound of that sigh. Penelope needed to stick it out if she was going to make anything of this venture. "What was the best wedding you ever attended?"

Penelope groaned. "I don't even want to think about weddings."

That didn't seem auspicious, but before Wes could change the subject, she reached for her beer, took a drink and straightened in her chair.

"It was when I was six. Cousin Jason was the groom. He's part of the branch of my family that lives in San Diego. We all drove down for the wedding. They had it on a sailing ship—one of those old-fashioned sloops that offer dinner cruises. It was so pretty, just the family and close friends. They held the ceremony on deck as the sun set, and then the sails were lit up with fairy lights while we ate and danced. I felt like I was in a story book. I never wanted it to end."

"Sounds amazing," Wes said. Her face was transformed by the memory. Softer somehow, but she was energized, too.

"Jason and Pauline were so happy. Like, over the moon. Everything the crew did thrilled them. They loved the music, and the food, and each other. We were all happy, too. You have to understand. I have a big family. Things don't always go smoothly when we all get together, but that night was really special."

"And you want to create nights like that for your clients," he guessed.

"That's right. I don't think I'm going to for Olivia. I'm not sure it's possible to cheer her up."

"Trying to control someone else's emotions seems like a setup, don't you think?" he asked. "Maybe it's more important to work on your own state of mind."

"Maybe." Penelope didn't sound convinced. "What about you? Are you making yourself happy?"

Wes snorted before he could stop himself. "For the moment, yes, but for the long term? That's the million-dollar question."

"Because your family wants you to work in their business?"

He nodded. "All I've ever wanted to do was be a fishing guide, but suddenly Dad wants me to be CEO."

"Can't you tell him you don't want to do it?"

"Sounds like they're in a jam." He didn't want to get into it. "You're lucky you're on good terms with your mom."

Penelope shrugged, tracing a finger over the label on her beer bottle. "I'm kind of mad at my mom," she admitted. "Which isn't fair at all. Mom's great and she did a lot for me. It's just… she's changed."

"How so?"

"She was always so steady. So dependable. I could pop home any time, and she'd be there. When Dad died, he left a pretty substantial insurance policy, and Mom was able to keep being a homemaker like she'd always been. She volunteered a little. Had a group of friends. I thought she was happy."

"Was she lonely?"

"I guess so. Two years ago she met Chris Benson when she was on vacation, and she married him a few months back. Now they're living it up in Costa Rica. Chris isn't like the rest of us at all. My whole family lives in California—dozens of us. It's our home. We're settled here. Chris never even gave it a chance."

"Does he make your mom happy?"

"Yes," Penelope grumbled. "She's like a kid again. Trying new things. Going out dancing, hiking, camping. They're building a house there. Off the grid. Doesn't that sound like something I should be doing?"

"Do you want to live off the grid in Costa Rica?" he asked curiously.

"No." Penelope laughed. "But I want to have a few adventures. And I want… I want someone to love. I want kids. My best friends—Emma and Ava—are both married now. They're wives. Their businesses are thriving. Emma's pregnant. And here I am babysitting grumpy second-tier celebrities. Alone."

His heart went out to her. He'd thought he was getting somewhere in life finally. Ready to start an adventure of his own. Then came the phone call from his parents. The guilt trip. This vacation felt like a last gasp of air before he was dragged under.

"At least you have a home," he said.

"Don't you?"

"No." He wasn't sure how to explain it. "I travel too much." That wasn't really it, though. To his surprise, Wes began telling Penelope about his boarding-school years. The way he would come home and take up residence in a corner of his parents' exercise room, where all their pieces of equipment got much more space than he was allotted. "My mother's off-season wardrobe always filled the closet. I lived out of my suitcase."

"I noticed you're still doing that. There's plenty of room in the closet here, you know."

"I never want to overstep."

Penelope looked at him. "You're not overstepping, Wes. You're my guest. That room is all for you. That's what I designed it for. When I painted it and bought the furniture, I couldn't wait to have someone come and stay. I'm glad it's you."

A small, uncomfortable silence lingered between

them.

"I'm glad it's me, too," he said finally, careful not to read too much into what she'd said. "You're a terrific hostess."

"Thank you."

"I want a family, too, you know," he admitted, surprising himself all over again. He didn't think he'd ever said that out loud.

"Really?"

He nodded. "I've never found a woman who wanted the same things I do. And now it's too late."

"Is it?" she asked, a little breathlessly.

Wes took her hand. Maybe it wasn't. Maybe...

He leaned over, gently tugged her closer and closed the gap between them, hesitating to make sure she was okay with this. He was breaking his own rules again—and Penelope's. She'd said she couldn't afford an entanglement right now.

Yet here he was trying to kiss her all the same.

Wes stopped, close but not bridging the gap between them. He had to let Penelope make the final move.

When she eased forward and her mouth met his, something shifted low inside him, and the desire he'd kept pent up all day long surged through him. God, he wanted Penelope. His hand slid into her thick curls as their kiss continued. She tasted so good. She was vital, interesting, sexy.

When she pulled back, he held his breath.

"I think… I think I'd better call it a night," Penelope said.

Disappointment flooded him, but Wes knew she was being smart. Why start something they couldn't finish?

"Good night," she said, standing a little unsteadily.

"Night."

CHAPTER 5

*P*ENELOPE LAY AWAKE for hours thinking about that kiss, wondering what would have happened if she hadn't pulled away when she had. If she'd given into her real feelings.

Why was she holding Wes at arm's length? She never used to get so tied up in knots around men. She'd had two serious relationships and always trusted her gut when it came to them. Wes was a good guy. He shared her favorite hobby. Was planning to turn it into a career, just like she once had.

Penelope admitted to herself that she'd put off thinking about men altogether since the incident with Roger Atlas and her banishment from the *Amphitrite*. She hadn't done so consciously, but here she was all the same, more than a year later.

Single.

Her attraction to Wes was visceral. It made sense given all they had in common. Watching Wes catching fish, moving around the *Amphitrite* so at home in her world, was heady stuff. Still, she kept backing away.

Was she afraid of him?

Or was she afraid of what Uncle Dan would say if he was still alive?

Penelope wrestled with the question, her memory returning again and again to the day she'd defied Dan's orders and tried to climb aboard the *Amphitrite* again. She'd showed up unannounced, knowing he was hosting a set of guests they'd hosted many times before. The Adlers were a friendly family—three generations who returned to Fisherman's Point year after year.

Penelope had hoped she could slip aboard, quietly announce her presence to her uncle and get right to work like she always did when they hosted return guests. The Adlers were already aboard when she showed up, and they greeted her happily, but Uncle Dan had taken one look at her and started yelling.

"Get off the boat! Get… off… this… boat!" He'd come at her, hands up as if he meant to shove her overboard. Penelope had backpedaled fast and somehow clambered over the gunwale and back onto the dock. She remembered the Adlers' shocked faces. Their mouths O-shaped with surprise.

What had he told them when he'd cast off and roared out of the harbor, the *Amphitrite* going well above the speed limit?

That she was a danger to everyone around her?

That she attracted chaos?

That she couldn't be trusted even with old fishing

friends?

Penelope rolled over and covered her head with her pillow, shame expanding to fill her body.

She hadn't done anything wrong—except be a woman, but that was always the problem, wasn't it? She'd had to convince Uncle Daniel she was as good as a man, and for a while he'd bought it, but she'd been living on borrowed time.

Roger Atlas had exposed her for what she really was. A target. A liability in her uncle's eyes. A weak link. Uncle Dan couldn't stand that, and he'd banned her from the boat.

Banned her from his life, too.

The worst of it was that he'd left her no way to redeem herself. She couldn't change the fact that she was a woman.

Didn't want to.

Penelope flopped onto her back in frustration, her mind going in circles. In the end she came to the same conclusion she always did. There was nothing she could have done to make things right between her and her uncle. It wasn't her fault he hadn't taken the necessary steps to leave the *Amphitrite* to someone else.

Now he was gone, but she was still alive. Surely, she got to call the shots as far as fishing was concerned.

So why couldn't she get past the feeling that Uncle Dan was still watching her? Still judging her and finding her wanting?

She finally fell asleep around one thirty in the morning and woke up at three when Olivia and her entourage came home. By the time they'd settled in, she had only twenty minutes before she was due up again. She got up dispiritedly and headed for the bathroom, wondering how she'd ever make it through the long day ahead of her.

Luckily, she and Wes had a system now. They both worked to get ready and gather what they needed for a morning on the ocean. Once in her car, she breathed a sigh of relief, but she didn't know what to say to Wes. He was quiet, too.

Once she'd parked at the marina, they headed in the low light for the *Amphitrite*'s berth, but they hadn't gotten far when a man she recognized came toward them down the dock. Mac MacArthur was sixty-five, deeply tanned from years in the sun and walked with a swagger. His beer-belly resembled a full-term pregnancy. Penelope had known him since she was a girl.

"Penelope Rider. Just the woman I was looking for."

"Oh, yeah? What can I do for you, Mac?" She hoped he wouldn't waylay them for long. Their time on the water would be short enough.

"Wondering if you're ready to sell."

"Sell?" she repeated stupidly. "Sell what?"

"The *Amphitrite*. I told your uncle I would take care of it when he was gone."

"I'm not planning to sell it."

Mac talked right over her. "I'm expanding my operation. I've had a couple of banner years, and I can't keep up with the demand. My brother's kid is signing on to help full-time. Just hired six more crew members, too. I need another boat."

"Well, I'm afraid—"

"Your uncle wanted me to have the *Amphitrite*, especially after what happened to you. We should have gone into business together years ago, but now it's too late for that. I'll pay you top dollar, of course."

"It's not for sale." Speaking up to be heard, her words were sharp in the still air.

Mac frowned. Looked her up and down. "Of course it's for sale. You know how your uncle felt."

He took in the gear she was carrying. Wes behind her. "You're not fishing on the *Amphitrite*, are you?"

"Of course I am. Uncle Dan left it to me."

"He never wanted you to set foot on it again!"

"Dan's not here."

"But I am." Mac stepped closer, but before he could go on, Wes came to her defense.

"If anyone should be expanding her business, it's Penelope. She's the best guide I've ever fished with, and that's saying a lot. I've been all over the world. Fished with experts. If anyone asked me to recommend a trip, I'd put Penelope at the top of the list."

"Penelope puts on weddings," Mac said. "And people like you are the reason her uncle put his foot down.

You have to sell the Amphitrite," he said to Penelope. "I've been patient. I don't know what your game is playing hard to get. Your uncle wouldn't be proud of you today."

Penelope tried to swallow down her anger. She didn't want to be discourteous to an old family friend, but Mac knew exactly where her weaknesses lay and his words twisted like a knife in her heart. "Uncle Dan knew I'm a capable guide."

"He knew you're a woman, and a woman's not safe on a boat like that."

Wes stepped between them and drew himself up to his full height. "The Amphitrite is not for sale," he said in a deceptively calm voice. Mac's gaze sharpened and he took a step back.

"You want me to call the police, Penelope? You just say the word, they'll be here in a minute."

"I do not want you to call the police. Wes is my guest. I'm taking him fishing. That's all that's going on here."

"Fine. Be that way. Break your uncle's heart wherever he might be," he growled. "But you won't get a better offer than what I was prepared to pay and if you get hurt again, don't come crying to me." He stalked off down the dock and disappeared onto his own vessel.

Penelope searched for something to say that wouldn't betray the cascade of emotions inside her. How dare Mac talk to her that way? Why were the men who'd once championed her now lining up to make her feel small?

"I should have told him where to get off," she said. "I should go find him and tell him right now."

"Do you know that guy well?"

"He was one of Dan's best friends. He helped my uncle teach me to fish!" Mac's betrayal had her nearly in tears. "He knows how good I am. He knows the Amphitrite should belong to me."

"Let's talk this over on the water." Wes led her to the boat. "You're not going to change his mind by arguing with him."

"What do you suggest? Tossing him into the ocean?"

"Nothing as drastic as that." He climbed aboard, waited for her to follow and began moving around the boat as if it was his own. Penelope's hands were shaking as she took the wheel, but she was able to maneuver the Amphitrite out of the harbor and down the coast.

Memories flooded her mind of all the times she'd come this way growing up. Not all her trips with Dan were for work. On days off, they came out with friends to fish and hang out. Mac was a part of those memories. When she was a child, all Dan's companions had cheered her on as she grew in skill and accomplishment.

Now they thought she should sell her boat.

It wasn't fair. More than that—it was wrong.

"Don't you dare sell the Amphitrite to that man," Wes said when she finally cut the engine.

"I won't." She wasn't selling to anyone, no matter what Mac or anyone else said. "You should have let me go after him."

"Fishing communities are all the same—small and interdependent. You piss off one guy and you'll end up pissing everyone off. You depend on these people, Pen. You don't want to become an outsider here. Besides, sounds like he worries about you."

She already felt like an outsider, the way the other fishermen looked at her. She hated their pity. "I don't care if he does. I can handle myself. I can handle him, too!"

"Can you? He was pushing all your buttons and you were letting him."

He was right. She supposed she should have seen this coming. Mac and Uncle Dan were thick as thieves and her uncle had obviously told him everything. Mac must think he was carrying out Dan's dying wish.

It still hurt that he agreed with her uncle, though. Had he fought for her at all? Had he reminded Dan of how capable she was? How much she loved the Amphitrite?

She hadn't helped her cause by staying away for so long, had she? Did everyone in the fishing community think she was washed up?

And what if she screwed up this wedding and was forced to sell the Amphitrite? She didn't think she could bear that. A tear spilled down her cheek. And another.

Penelope scrubbed them away and stalked off to get her gear, wiping her face with the tail of her t-shirt. They were out here to fish, right? They needed to get fishing.

"Thank you for telling Mac the Amphitrite wasn't for sale," she said stiffly when she returned.

"That's what friends do. They back each other up."

"Is that what you are? My friend?"

Wes set down his rod. Came to face her and put his hands on her shoulders. "Damn right I am. You know I want to be more than that, too, but no matter if we get closer or not, I've got your back, Penelope Rider. You understand me?"

"I guess so."

WHAT HAD HAPPENED on board the Amphitrite that had spooked all the men around Penelope so badly?

Penelope's tepid response to his assurances told him she didn't really believe him. Wes was trying not to take that personally. Something had happened and her uncle's reaction to it had broken her heart. Now she was afraid to trust anyone, especially a man she barely knew.

Wes cast his line and thought over everything she'd said so far. There'd been an incident with a paying customer, after which Penelope's uncle had banned her from the boat. She'd thought he'd change his will and leave the Amphitrite to someone else, but he hadn't. After she'd inherited it, she'd been afraid to take it out on her own.

Now her uncle's friend, who'd previously supported her love of the sea and fishing, thought she should sell her boat to him.

Had she screwed something up so badly on board they thought she was a danger to herself?

No, Wes thought. He'd bet anything it had to do with that guest. The one she'd begun to tell him about and then switched stories mid-stream. Whatever had happened had scared Dan and Mac so badly they'd rather ban Penelope from fishing than take the risk of it happening again.

There was an obvious possibility but Penelope had told him she'd never taken the Amphitrite out alone. If her uncle had been aboard at the time of the incident with this unruly guest, how could anything truly bad have happened to her? It must have been something else.

When the silence between them got too long, Wes spoke up.

"I had to give up a boat once." Hardly anyone knew about his failure with the Loose Cannon and he felt awkward talking about it, but he figured Penelope would understand if anyone could.

"You did?"

He nodded. "I was right out of college. Thought I knew everything. My folks wanted me to go into the family business but I persuaded them to give me the summer off. I spent it with a friend of mine fishing in southeast Asia. Two months in, I persuaded myself we knew enough to go into business for ourselves. I tried to get a loan from a bank, but that didn't work. Despite my parents' money, I had no track record. My buddy, Kennedy, had better connections."

Wes couldn't believe he was actually telling her all this. He concentrated on the rod in his hands and the waves off the side of the boat.

"Kennedy secured the loan and I signed my name to it. We got the boat, put together a website and waited for some customers to show up."

"Did you have a marketing plan?" Penelope asked.

"Hell, no." Wes laughed. "We didn't know a damn thing. I mean, we told our friends about our plans and asked them to pass on the word. We had a couple of social media accounts and posted a bunch of photos of us fishing on the boat. It never occurred to either of us that it could take months—or years—to build up the business enough to support ourselves, never mind pay back the loan."

"Oh, no."

"Oh, yes," Wes said. "Summer ended. My parents wanted me to come home. I didn't want to, but we were desperate for cash. Kennedy stayed with the boat. I went back and tried to learn the telecommunications business. I was sending him cash each month, getting a taste of what it had been like for my parents to support me. He kept throwing photos up on social media, but now they were of him partying on the boat, bringing girls around, getting wasted, that kind of thing. I was pissed."

"I bet. You were working. He was playing."

"Exactly. And I was living at home, too. Sleeping in my mom's exercise room. Try bringing a girl back to that. Not sexy."

Penelope laughed, then bit her lip. "Sorry."

"Don't be. I deserve your mockery. I was so damn dumb."

"You were what—twenty-two?"

He nodded. "That's no excuse, though. My parents run a multi-million-dollar business. You'd think I would have picked up some common sense. Anyway," he went on before she could try to make him feel better, "one day there was a knock on our door, which was odd enough—my folks live in a penthouse and no one comes up without the doorman giving them access. What was even stranger was that when my Dad answered the door, he didn't recognize the man on the other side."

Penelope wasn't paying attention to her rod anymore. "Who was it?"

"Kennedy's connection. The man who gave us the loan, who turned out not to be affiliated with a credit union. That's what my twenty-two-year-old brain had assumed when Kennedy told me he was with an *alternative finance institution*."

"He was a loan shark?"

"You got it."

"What about your friend? Didn't he sign for the loan,

too?"

"Turned out he was getting a kickback for having brought my business to this guy. Anyway, the man laid out the details of the deal to my dad. Let him know the consequences of non-payment. Dad took out his checkbook and his fountain pen. You should have seen the look on the guy's face when he did that," Wes added. "He said he'd prefer cash, of course."

"Of course."

"Anyway, they made arrangements. Dad paid off the bill. The next week he sold the Loose Cannon. Managed to make a profit on it, actually." Wes shook his head. "That's my dad all over."

"There must have been hell to pay after that."

Wes looked down and realized he was gripping the rod so tightly, his knuckles were white. He tried to release the tension. "No," he said. "No yelling. No punishments. No demands that I pay him anything."

"Really?" Penelope's brows furrowed.

"All he said was, 'Now you owe me.'" The four words still twisted Wes' gut every time he thought about them, because he'd never repaid that debt—until now.

Penelope let her line go lax. "That's not fair."

"Of course it is. That boat cost a pretty penny."

"You said he made a profit selling it. Even if he wanted to charge you something to teach you a lesson, he could have laid out terms and made you sign an agreement. You could have paid him back over a number of years. Instead, he's been holding you hostage."

Wes shrugged. "And bankrolling my really cushy life."

"Is that why you haven't started your guiding business yet?" she asked. "Because you're afraid as soon as you do, he'll take that support away?"

Her words took the breath out of his lungs. Was he that much of a coward?

No, Wes told himself. He'd learned from his past mistakes. This time, he'd made a very careful plan.

"I'll start my business in six months, when I'm ready."

"Really? Sounds to me like he's calling in that debt he thinks you owe him."

Wes's fingers clenched again. He couldn't answer, so instead he reeled in his line. "We'd better turn around if we're going to get back in time."

WES HAD BEEN so eager to dodge her questions, he'd gotten them home a half-hour early. Penelope knew she'd pushed him too hard, but it was easier to focus on someone else's problems rather than her own.

She was looking forward to running upstairs to take a quick shower before her day began. She'd need to spend the rest of it catering to Olivia's every whim, and she wanted to be mentally prepared.

When she went to pull into the driveway, however,

the parking area was already full of trucks. She had to do a quick maneuver that got her back out onto the street and drive a block away before she could find parking.

"What's going on?" Wes asked.

"I don't know." She intended to find out right away.

When they reached the house, she groaned. All the first-floor furniture was stacked outside and her heart was in her throat as she opened the door and went to see what was happening. Was Amber making good on her threat to put all her furniture in storage, or was there an even bigger problem?

There were workmen everywhere. Dropcloths laid on every square inch of floor. The distinct scent of paint filled the air.

Penelope hustled down the hall to the front room, but when she got there, she stopped so fast Wes collided with her from behind.

"What are you doing?" Her words caught in her throat, but Amber and Olivia heard them anyway from where they were standing in consultation with one of the workmen.

"Don't you love it?" Olivia sashayed their way, throwing her hands wide to encompass the room. Every inch of the walls and ceiling was now a Pepto-Bismol colored pink.

"It's Olivia's new aesthetic," Amber called out. "It's going to be a hit. Super feminine. Super aggressive. It sums up the zeitgeist of the times."

"You painted my house?" How had they even got up early enough to do that? They'd been out until three in the morning. Penelope's voice still wasn't obeying her. She tried again. "You're not allowed to paint my house!"

"Watch your tone." Amber stepped between her and Olivia. "You gave us carte blanch to use your property as the backdrop for Olivia's very important wedding. You signed a contract giving us permission to modify the house, its contents and its surroundings to suit our purposes. Olivia woke up early today with a new idea."

"I didn't say you could paint my house!"

"Jerome? Contract!" Amber snapped, holding out a hand. A young man tapped at his tablet, then placed it in her palm. Amber scrolled a moment, then turned the screen Penelope's way.

"Client shall have exclusive use of the house, its contents and environs, and may adjust, rearrange, reorder, renovate, remodel and resituate any or all as the Client's needs demand."

"I didn't sign that!" She couldn't have, could she?

Amber was already scrolling again. There was her signature, plain as day.

"I didn't know you'd actually damage my property."

"We didn't damage it; we improved it."

"Improved it?" Her voice was sliding toward a higher register again. She'd picked the sweetest shade of faintly apricot paint for these rooms. It had golden undertones that lit up like a sunrise when the light hit it in the morning. Now all of it was under a thick layer of syrupy pinkness that made her want to throw up.

Penelope turned, her hands outstretched to encompass the horror of it and her words caught in her throat all over again. "No," she cried when she could speak again. "What did you do?" She strode toward the fireplace where her favorite painting hung. The textured brush strokes were coated with a uniform wash of pink. "That was an original. It's irreplaceable!" She turned on Amber and Olivia, and for once had the pleasure of seeing them both flinch. "Why would you destroy something beautiful like that?"

Olivia lifted her chin. "I'm an artist. I do what I feel. And what I feel right now is attacked and belittled. I'm not sure I want my name attached to this wedding venue of yours."

Fear swamped Penelope's outrage. If Olivia bailed now, she'd be stuck with the cost of painting all over again and she wouldn't be able to make this month's loan payment. For better or for worse, she needed this to work out.

She struggled against an urge to scream, closed her eyes and summoned every last vestige of patience she possessed.

"I assume you'll put it all to rights when you're done—including the painting?" She opened her eyes again, clinging onto the fragments of her self-esteem. It was clear Olivia knew how badly she needed her and meant to milk that for all it was worth.

"That's not in the contract," Amber said.

Olivia smirked. "You really should read the fine print if you want to be a businesswoman."

Penelope turned on her heel, nearly bumping into Wes, who was still behind her, looking like he had a lot to say, but not saying a word.

"Where are you going?" Amber called after her.

"Coffee."

"That's a good idea. I'd like—"

"There's nothing in the contract that says I have to fetch you beverages." Trailed by Wes, Penelope kept moving, savoring the tiny victory, knowing as she did so how small it really was. After all, Amber could easily send Jerome.

"By the way, we missed you last night." Olivia followed them down the hall. "I called the people with your ticket numbers up to the stage to meet the band. Turned out you gave them to someone else."

When Penelope turned, she saw a flash of something like anger in Olivia's face—or maybe hurt. Was that what this was all about? Was Olivia mad she hadn't made it to the concert?

"I gave them to some of my very good friends. I'm glad they got to meet you. I was in bed. I'd been up since four in the morning." Her excuse sounded lame to her own ears.

"Guess that's what happens when you get old." Olivia flounced away again.

Wes caught Penelope by the arm. "Coffee," he reminded her. She allowed herself to be led outdoors. "Give me your keys. I'll drive."

She didn't even fight him. She was far too furious to take the wheel, and what was worse, that helpless feeling was back. She'd signed a damn contract giving these people permission to destroy her home and she'd already poisoned her relationship with them so much that at the end of this debacle, who knew if she'd get any business out of it or not?

"Are you going to be okay?" he asked when they were on their way.

"I don't know."

"CAN I ASK you something?" Wes asked when they'd made it to Cups & Waves, had gotten their coffee and were settled in a corner table tucked out of the way. He liked the clean, spare lines of the shop with its wide wooden floorboards, cool cream walls and turquoise trim, but the soothing interior was doing little to calm Penelope.

He didn't blame her for being furious with Amber and Olivia. If he'd had his way, he'd have bodily thrown them and their entire retinue into the street the minute he saw the damage to the place, but he knew Penelope needed their business. He'd decided to step back and let her handle things.

"Why are you letting Olivia get away with this?"

"I signed a contract apparently. One I didn't read closely enough."

"I mean why do you need their money so badly? What they're doing is unreasonable. You could kick them out and fight in court if they pursued a claim—unless you're broke."

Penelope clasped her drink with both hands but didn't lift it. "I am broke. Uncle Dan took a loan out against the house about seven years back to buy the Amphitrite. I'm still paying that off, along with the renovation costs." She ducked her head, probably thinking about all that would need to be repaired again. "I'm going to lose my boat if Olivia doesn't pay her bills in full. Even then, I'm going to be low on cash. I need this to work."

He wasn't sure what to tell her. She seemed to have made an enemy of Olivia now, and he had a feeling Olivia didn't get over her grudges easily.

When his phone buzzed in his pocket, he pulled it out, saw his sister's name and sighed. "I have to take this. Sorry."

Penelope waved him away and Wes took the call, getting up from the table and crossing the café to stand near the door.

"We need to talk," Grace said without preamble.

"What did you do?" He was too worried about Penelope to mince words with his sister.

"I didn't do anything. That's the whole problem!"

"That's not what Mom and Dad said."

"They're accusing me of embezzlement, which is rich, considering they're—"

"Embezzlement?" Wes cut across her. Maybe he wasn't the smartest businessman, but he knew this kind of thing could tear businesses—and families—apart. No wonder his parents were beside themselves. Abbott Enterprises depended on its good name to hold onto its market share. Wrongdoing within the company, by the founders' daughter, would be seized on by their competition and trumpeted to the world.

"I didn't—"

"You can't call me." If his parents wanted him to step in as CEO, he had to be untainted by this. They'd hired his sister, which made them suspect. As of right now, he was the only one with his hands clean and they needed to stay that way.

"Wes!"

"I'm hanging up now." There'd never been much love lost between him and his sister. Grace had never gone to boarding school. Her childhood bedroom remained an altar to the girl she'd once been, although she'd moved out long ago. She'd already taken the bulk of his parents' affection. She'd gotten the bulk of their company, too. Wasn't that enough?

He tapped the screen and pocketed the phone, bile burning in his throat.

"Everything okay?" Penelope asked when he rejoined her.

"It's fine," he lied.

It wasn't fine.

Penelope was right. His dad was about to call in his debt and now that he knew what Grace had done, Wes couldn't refuse. Abbott Enterprises was his parents' life work and someone needed to take charge of it. Someone who'd remained above the fray until this point.

Him.

Forget buying a boat, becoming a guide and spending his life on the water. Forget all his dreams.

He took a long drink of coffee, so lost in his thoughts he barely noticed Penelope was just as lost in hers.

CHAPTER 6

"*D*ON'T EVEN LOOK," Wes whispered, shielding her from any view of the great room when he and Penelope made their way downstairs the next morning. He'd kept her away from the house for hours the previous day, making her take him on a walk in the redwoods, followed by dinner at a pizza restaurant nearby. Despite the worries that seemed to lay heavy on his shoulders, Wes had been an attentive companion. He'd been content to see Seahaven through her eyes and had been happy enough with their low-key hike and the family-style restaurant.

Back at home, he'd rushed her upstairs to her third-floor apartment. Neither Amber nor Olivia had come to find them. Penelope hoped they'd be as lucky this morning. She'd gotten little sleep last night and Wes looked tired, as well.

They made it out of the house without incident and drove to the marina. On board the Amphitrite, Penelope moved automatically, while Wes seemed to be striving for a balance between helpful and not overstepping his rank as guest and passenger. She finally took the wheel and steered them out of the harbor into open water.

When it was time for fishing, Wes said, "You seem a little calmer today."

"I've decided there's no use in dwelling on what happened yesterday," she said. "Olivia trashed my place to get back at me for not coming to her concert. She wanted a reaction and she got one. The more I react, the more she'll do to provoke me, so as far as I'm concerned what's done is done. I'll repaint when she's gone. It will only take me a day."

"Sounds smart."

"It's easy to say," she admitted. "Harder to stick to."

"I know what you mean, but I've decided that this morning the only thing I'm worrying about is catching fish. Bet I catch more than you today."

"I doubt it," she scoffed, more than happy to grasp at the distraction. "I've been fishing these waters my whole life."

"Want to place a friendly wager on it?"

"Sure. What are we betting?"

"Breakfast. Loser has to take the winner to whatever god-awful diner is open at four in the morning tomorrow."

Penelope laughed and he smiled in return. "Sunnyside Diner is actually pretty good," she told him. "Okay, you're on. Loser buys breakfast."

With the tension lessened, they cast their lines and

spent the next hour swapping stories. Wes told her about the time he'd stayed in a hostel in Thailand and had just gotten out of his lower bunk one morning when the whole structure imploded under the weight of the couple in the top bunk.

"I'd have been a pancake if I'd slept for thirty seconds longer," he finished up.

"That's crazy."

"It's better here. I wish I could stay and crew for you," Wes said. "I swear, the last few days have taught me I don't even have to be in charge to enjoy this life. As long as I get to spend my days on a boat, I'd be content."

"That might be fun."

Wes perked up. "Oh, yeah? You like spending time with me?"

She shrugged. "You aren't the worst."

"I'm not the worst?" He gave her a shove with his shoulder. "I'm the best fishing buddy you ever had. Admit it."

"I guess I can admit that," she said. "My uncle wasn't exactly a buddy, but he did teach me everything I know."

"Your uncle is in a different category. I'm talking pure camaraderie. Not relatives."

"In that case, you're number one."

Wes straightened, clearly pleased with the praise. He bumped her shoulder softly with his again. There wasn't much else he could do while each of them held a fishing pole. "You know what?" he asked. "I want to kiss you.

But I'm not going to, because I'm a man of my word."

Warmth suffused Penelope and the desire that had been simmering inside her since his arrival grew stronger. She couldn't help wondering what kissing him would be like. "You know what?" she heard herself say. "I want you to kiss me. I'm granting you permission."

"Now, you're talking."

Wes set the butt of his pole in one of the holders, careful to secure it, then waited for Penelope to do the same. Her hands shook a little as she managed it and she was afraid the moment would get awkward, but when he stepped close to her, drew her into his arms and brushed her mouth with his own, she forgot everything else.

Wes tasted like fresh air and salt water and as they kissed, she parted her lips to let him in, the ache of wanting to be even closer to him as sweet as sunshine.

She'd missed this kind of human contact. She had never been a loner and lately her days had been spent far too much alone. What she felt for Wes was uncomplicated. She wanted to stay right here in his arms. Wanted him to keep on kissing her. Wanted more than that.

But Wes was a guest. He wouldn't be around long.

"We'd better check our lines," she whispered against his mouth.

Wes slowly let her go. Penelope picked up her pole again, testing the play of the line. She hoped he couldn't see how much he'd affected her.

"I got a bite," she said.

"Me, too."

With that, their competitive spirits kicked in and for the next two hours they traded kisses, insults and laughter as they raced to beat each other. In the end, Wes won, but only by a single fish. Penelope allowed him to claim a victory kiss that had her wanting him even more.

"We're going to be late," she finally said, pushing him away and setting to the work of getting ready for their return trip.

Wes checked his phone. "You're right. We'll have to hustle if we're going to get home on time."

They got to work and soon enough they were underway. Penelope knew it was going to be tight, though. She made as good time as she dared, but they had to enter the harbor at a crawl and it always took time to secure the boat.

They worked together smoothly and Penelope realized that if she ever needed a crew member, she couldn't do better than Wes. He seemed to anticipate her movements and was always there to lend a hand. There was no way they'd make it on time, but they'd only be a few minutes late. Maybe Olivia would sleep in like she had the first day.

Wes went ahead of her to the car, carrying the cooler with the morning's catch. He'd cleaned and processed the fish like a pro and now they were ready to store away for use later.

Penelope stayed behind to check the *Amphitrite* one last time, before hurrying to catch up with him. She nearly groaned when she spotted Mac standing in her way.

"Hey," he said as she approached. "I want to talk to you."

"Can I give you a call later? I've got to be back at the house. I've got guests waiting for me." Penelope went to push past him, but Mac stepped in front of her, making it clear he meant for them to talk right now.

"What are you thinking, Penelope? Taking that guy out on the boat alone in the wee hours."

"He's a client. I'm taking him fishing. That's how all of this works." She tried to dodge around Mac's other side, but he was quicker than she'd imagined, and he got in her way again.

"Your uncle might be gone, but I'm still here. I can't protect you if you won't listen to reason."

"I didn't ask for your protection. I don't need it!"

"Really? That's not what Dan told me. That's not what you told the police!"

Penelope sucked in a breath, but Mac went on before she could protest.

"Your uncle cared about you. I care about you. You want to take the *Amphitrite* out, at least take one of your cousins to chaperone."

"Chaperone?" She wasn't some child.

"You keep inviting that guy out there alone, he'll take

142

what you don't give," Mac said. "And then I'll have to kill him. Is that what you want?"

"Jesus, Mac."

"Now you're swearing, too. What happened to you, Penelope? You used to be—" He cut off. "You never used to cause so much trouble."

He pushed past her, leaving Penelope reeling. *She* was causing trouble?

It was Roger Atlas who'd done that.

"Penelope," Wes called from her car. "We're late!"

Penelope started walking again although she didn't know how she was managing it. Her mind was full of memories of a fishing trip that had gone all wrong. Usually she kept them buried, and she didn't want to think about them now.

After all, she had plenty to worry about in the present.

"EVERYTHING ALL RIGHT?" Wes asked. He knew they were late, but Penelope was driving like they were being chased. She was frowning with concentration, hunched over the steering wheel, her shoulders tight. He'd seen Mac waylay her on the dock. What had the man said to her?

"It's fine," she said, but he knew it wasn't. He hoped she wasn't regretting their kisses. He sure wasn't.

"I'm here if you want to talk about it."

"I said it's fine."

Wes decided to leave her alone for now, especially since they were approaching the house. Just like yesterday, the place was swarming with workmen, although he was pretty sure there was a new batch of trucks outside.

Penelope swore under her breath and found a parking spot down the street. Hurrying back, Wes trailing behind her, she burst into the house and strode down the hall.

"Now what's going on?" She stopped short. At least this time Wes managed to stop, too, before colliding with her. He peered around her shoulders and groaned.

The kitchen was in ruins. Workmen were in the process of taking cabinets off the wall and dismantling the large island that separated the space from the living room.

"It's in the way," Amber asserted, stalking over to Penelope with purpose. "We need room for the band. We can't predict the weather, so we need room inside and out for the dancing."

"You can't—"

"Yes, we can," Amber overrode her. "You signed the contract, remember?"

"But—"

"Careful with those." Wes threaded his way through the women and reached the workmen in a couple of strides. "There better not be a scratch on anything in this kitchen. It needs to be reassembled perfectly."

"Can't get this counter off in one piece," one of the men said, jerking his head to indicate Penelope's granite countertop.

"You'll figure it out or you won't move it," Wes rejoined. He folded his arms and stood there, making it clear he was going to watch the whole operation. It was the least he could do. This was insane. There was no way it was legal for Amber and Olivia to dismantle Penelope's kitchen.

Penelope and Amber were still arguing.

"We can't fit eighty people on that deck," Amber was saying. "We need both spaces."

"Eighty people? The limit is forty; we've been over that. It's in the contract."

Amber shook her head. "Fine. Tell you what. We'll leave today. We can pack all this up and be out of here in half an hour. You'll never hear from us again—except when I send a review of this disaster to every publicist I know. You want this business shut down before you even open?"

"It's going to get shut down if I exceed my capacity."

"You know your neighbors, right? Who's going to report you?" When Penelope looked down, it was clear Amber had won the day. "I thought so," Amber said. "Kevin—be ready to rip up this flooring the minute the fixtures are out of here."

One of the workmen nodded, and Penelope stifled a cry. "You can't rip up these floors," she started, but Wes walked straight up to Amber. This had to stop. He couldn't threaten her with bodily harm, but he had an idea he hoped would prove more effective.

"You're going to rip out hardwood floors? Original hardwood floors? After what Kelly Leggett just posted?"

"What did Kelly Leggett just post?" Amber grabbed her phone and started scrolling. "Chelsea? Get me a summary of Kelly Leggett's feed—everything from the last month. What's she up to?" she hissed at Wes.

"You're probably too late if you haven't seen it already. She's started posting flash updates she wipes within minutes," Wes said.

Amber's eyes widened. "What? I haven't heard about that."

"She did a photo shoot. Just her, a bikini and a hardwood floor. Sexy as hell. Everyone's talking about it."

More scrolling. And frowning.

"You want to get on that craze, believe me." He pointed to the floors. "Everyone else is going to be rushing to install them. You're ten steps ahead of them."

"I guess."

"Ah." He nodded knowingly. "You're worried about the comparison. You're afraid people will think Olivia is being derivative. Kelly can pull off a hardwood floor. Maybe Olivia isn't up to it?"

"She's up to it." Amber looked up from her phone. "You think Olivia isn't as good as Kelly Leggett?"

"Not sure she's got the following." Wes shrugged.

"She's got the following. She eats people like Kelly Leggett for lunch." Amber shoved her phone in her pocket. "All right. Leave the floor. Did you hear me? Leave it. Get those cabinets out of there." She clapped her hands and went to hurry the workmen.

"Thank you," Penelope whispered when Wes went to her side.

"You don't mind I stepped in?"

"Are you kidding? Those floors are original to the house. I'd die if Amber ripped them out."

THANK GOD WES had stopped Amber from stealing her floors. Penelope wished she'd never booked Olivia Raquette. She was beginning to think she'd never make it through the week. Her house might not, either.

Eighty guests? How was she going to hide them?

Amber was right about one thing: Emma and Ava wouldn't complain, but that didn't mean someone else might, and then where would she be? What if she lost her permit to host guests?

"Why don't you head upstairs for a while and let me keep an eye on these people."

"I don't know. I'm afraid to let them out of my sight."

"If Olivia is doing some of this to get back at you, it'll be better if you're not around."

She didn't point out that they'd been ripping out her

kitchen before she walked in the door. It was too depressing to see all her hard work undone in this way, even if she'd be able to reassemble it later.

"By the way, where's the groom? I haven't heard a word about him."

"I don't know." And right now, she didn't care, either.

"Olivia?" Wes said more loudly. "When is your groom arriving?"

"Vincent?" Olivia trilled. "He's coming tomorrow."

"So we've got that to look forward to," Wes murmured.

"Yay, us."

Upstairs, Penelope had to admit it was a relief to be away from the chaos. On the other hand, she wasn't sure what to do with herself. Her phone buzzed just as she stepped out onto the deck. It was Ava calling. She looked up to see Ava was standing on her deck next door, waving at her excitedly.

"Perfect timing!" Ava pocketed her phone, and Penelope's stopped buzzing. She pocketed hers too and moved to where she could hear Ava better.

"What's going on?"

"You won't believe it. I ran into Fee this morning, and I remembered to ask her for a tour!"

That was interesting. Euphemia Harper, Fee for short, was the caretaker of Seahaven Castle—and, depending on who you asked, possibly the heir to it as well. The castle, once a local tourist attraction, was indefinitely closed to the public, but Penelope and her friends had long hoped to convince Fee to give them a private tour. "What did she say?"

"She's got time today if we're up for it. Emma can make it, but I wasn't sure if you could, and I didn't want to leave you out."

"Actually, today is perfect. I need an excuse to get out of Olivia's way for a bit."

"Really? That's terrific. I'll let her know and text you the plan."

"Great!" Penelope told herself it was the smart thing to do to get out of the house altogether, but she wasn't sure if she'd made the right call. Somehow she doubted she'd be able to enjoy the tour very much today, and any other time she was sure it would be fun.

Deciding it was too late to change her mind, she took a quick shower and changed. By the time she was done, Ava had texted her again.

They were to meet Fee in an hour at a café near Castle Beach, in the shadow of the castle itself. When Penelope texted Wes, he assured her he would stick around and keep an eye on Olivia and Amber.

I need to pay you back for all the fishing trips you're taking me on, anyway. Don't worry. You can trust me to keep Amber in check.

She probably could, Penelope decided. He'd done a better job at it than she had. She crept out of the house, met up with Ava and Emma and together they drove across town. Noah and Sam were conspicuously absent. Due to a proclamation by Fee's grandmother fifty years ago, men weren't allowed to set foot in the castle.

When they reached the café, they found Fee waiting for them. She was a young woman with wild red hair that fell past her shoulders. She waved them over to the table she'd saved for them. When they took their seats, she asked for their orders. She crossed to the counter when she had them, struggling to corral her hair into a ponytail as she went, her curls springing out as fast as she could round them up.

Ava nudged Penelope and pointed at a man who had just entered the building and was heading for the counter, too. "Isn't that James Kane?"

Penelope leaned forward in her seat. She'd only ever seen the man in photos, but his sharp, formidable features were hard to mistake. James was legally the heir to Seahaven Castle, even though Fee was the current caretaker. The details were fuzzy to Penelope, but she knew James and Fee normally kept their distance from each other.

"I think it is. Do you think there will be a problem?"

Emma shook her head. "I don't think things are that bad between them."

Emma's husband, Noah, was the only one they knew who'd actually spoken to James. Around the time Noah met Emma, he'd taken a photograph of James surfing

Castle Beach. He'd been able to sell it to *SurfWorld* magazine, which had used it for a cover.

"Didn't Noah say James told him he was in town only temporarily? Why is he still here?"

"I don't know," Emma said.

"I wonder where he really lives," Penelope said. His comings and goings seemed as mysterious as everything else about him.

Fee, still struggling with her hair, hadn't noticed James yet. James had definitely spotted her, though, and his expression softened.

"Did you see that?" Penelope turned to her friends.

"See what?" Emma had glanced down at her phone. She was texting someone. Noah, maybe? Ava was looking at Fee.

"I swear that woman's curls give me an inferiority complex." She touched her auburn hair.

Penelope turned back to James, but he'd schooled his expression into something far more neutral. Had she actually seen something different before? She wasn't sure, and the moment had passed.

"Never mind," she said.

Fee spotted James. He quickly averted his gaze, pretending he hadn't seen her.

Fee turned her back on him. Penelope wondered if they'd greet one another at all.

When the customer ahead of Fee took his order and walked away, it became impossible for the other two to pretend they hadn't seen each other. Fee said something. James answered. They exchanged a few words. Penelope couldn't hear what they said, but it didn't seem like more than the most basic of pleasantries. She struggled with the urge to cross the café and tell them both to smarten up. Their lives were tangled up with Seahaven Castle. Shouldn't they be working together to ensure its future?

Especially if James felt something for Fee?

A few minutes later he left the café, and Fee came back to the table with their orders. Penelope wondered if she should mention what she'd seen and decided against it. After all, she could only guess at what James was thinking. Maybe he was just being sympathetic about Fee's struggle with her unruly hair.

Fee passed out their drinks. "Did you see James Kane? God, he drives me crazy. He never says anything about the elephant in the room."

"You mean the castle?" Ava asked.

"If he's here to claim it, why doesn't he say so? Then I could sort out my own life. Right now I'm just stuck waiting to see what he'll do."

"Have you asked him?" Emma asked.

"No." Fee rolled her eyes. "Have you seen the guy? I keep telling myself to confront him, but whenever he comes around, I freeze up. I can barely string two sensible words together. He's so... intense. He's this hero to everyone around here, when as far as I can tell, he's done nothing except surf. He holds my whole future in his hands, and he says hi and bye and comes and goes and tells me nothing!"

"You need to have it out with him once and for all," Emma advised her. "There's nothing scary about James Kane as far as I can tell."

"You don't think so?" Fee groaned. "Maybe I'm just afraid of what I'll hear. The castle is my home. What if he wants me to leave? What will I do then? I've never had another job."

"The skills you've used to run the castle would transfer to other jobs," Penelope assured her.

"It would be disappointing to move from a castle to an apartment," Emma added sympathetically, "but if you regained control over your life in the process, wouldn't that be worth it?"

"I guess." Fee didn't sound too sure. "You can tell me after you see it."

"Maybe James wouldn't kick you out, even if he did take possession of it," Penelope said. "Maybe he'd want you to stay on as caretaker." She was thinking about the way he'd looked at Fee when they were standing at the counter.

"I don't know about that. Want to head over there now?" Fee asked. "I got our coffee to go."

They trouped out of the café and up two long flights of steep concrete steps that led to the top of the bluff where Seahaven Castle was perched—a climb that left Penelope a little out of breath. They crossed a grassy area to the castle gates. Hugely oversized wooden doors barred the entry through the curtain wall that made a square around the inner keep. Fee took an enormous key out of her purse, unlocked them and tugged with all her might to open one. Awe filled Penelope as they passed through the arched entranceway and she looked up at the tall keep and the huge curtain walls surrounding it. Fee shut the doors behind them with a solid thump.

"In the old days, the medieval faire was held here." Fee gestured to the wide space between the keep and the outer walls. "There were food and craft stalls. On the far side of the keep, a stage would be set up where musical groups played. They had wandering minstrels and jugglers and clowns. Games and little shows to watch. There was even jousting in the field out back." She led them across the way to the keep, a three-story stone building with a wide main facade and a wing. The entrance led into a large foyer, with high ceilings and paneled walls.

"That's a cloakroom." Fee pointed to her left. "There's the kitchen." She pointed to another door across the way. "It's got its own staircase that leads straight to the formal dining hall on the second floor. There's a huge basement beneath our feet, but it contains only the wine cellar and storage, no dungeons." She smiled.

"What a shame," Ava joked.

"This is the main gallery." Fee headed to the right,

into a long, wide hall, with oil portraits of past members of the Kane family. The gallery ended in an enormous room, where Fee told them receptions could be held. "This is one of my favorite parts of the castle," she said, leading them through another door into a large, glassed-in room filled with tropical plants. "It's called the fernery. Don't you love it?"

"It's amazing," Penelope said. There were a lot of ferns, but there were many other plants, too. It was like stepping into a jungle, warm and tropical with sunlight streaming through the large windows.

"I'll show you the kitchen." Fee led them back the way they'd come. When she opened the door to the enormous kitchen, Emma gasped, and Penelope had to bite back a laugh.

"I want this kitchen," Emma said. "Oh, my goodness, Fee. The things you could do with a setup like this!"

"I know, right?" Fee said wistfully. "It must have been amazing in the old days."

"You've never thrown a party or something?" Emma was trailing around the room, touching the industrial-sized ovens and the miles of countertops.

Fee shook her head. "At the most there were four of us. Bethany, Lenore, Jeannette and me."

Penelope remembered hearing about Fee's family from Ava, but she didn't remember all the details. "You were Jeannette's ward?" she ventured.

"That's right. I called her Mom. Bethany was Grandma, and Lenore was Aunt Lenore, but I wasn't really related to any of them. Jeannette didn't adopt me. And we didn't entertain on a large scale," she added. "Now all of them are gone."

"You could entertain now," Penelope said.

"I guess I could." She didn't seem certain, though, and Penelope wondered what was holding her back. Was she afraid James would find out and put an end to it? "Let's go upstairs." Fee led the way up a steep staircase that opened through a door in the panelled walls to the dining hall.

Every room was bigger than the last, Penelope thought.

"You could host the whole town here," Ava said.

"Not quite, but several hundred people do fit in here," Fee told them proudly. She took them to see a library that had all of them sighing with longing, then another gallery, this one filled with landscape paintings, then a drawing room and a curved reading room with huge windows that sat above the fernery.

"Where does that door lead?" Penelope asked.

Fee smiled. "That's one of the towers." She opened the door and ushered them inside, where a spiral staircase curved out of sight. "Go on up."

They did so. Penelope loved the feel of the old stone steps under her feet. On the next level, a desk and chair snugged in under a window, the steps continuing to circle above it.

"You can get out onto the roof up there, but first I'll show you the third floor." Fee opened a door. They exited the tower into a master bedroom.

"Is this where you sleep?" Ava asked in hushed tones. It was a beautiful room, with views inland over the tall curtain walls.

"For now," Fee said. "It's going to be hard to give it up when James decides he wants the place. There's a second tower accessible only from this room." She pointed to a door near the end of the room. "And if you come this way"—she led them through a walk-in closet out into a hall—"you can reach the rest of the bed-rooms."

They peeked into each one in turn before Fee said, "Let's go out on the roof." She took them to yet another staircase. Penelope had long since gotten turned around. Were they over the kitchen and dining hall? She thought so. When they stepped onto the roof, she forgot everything else. The 360-degree view of Seahaven and the ocean was spectacular.

"Look at the surfers," Ava cried.

They were tiny seen from this height. Was James among them? Penelope couldn't pick him out if he was.

"Look at the Leaf!" Emma pointed to the streets near the heart of town that appeared in the shape of a leaf on maps of Seahaven—and from this vantage point.

"There's the marina," Penelope said, pointing into

the distance.

"There's the pier," Ava said.

It took some time for them to exhaust the town's landmarks, but they finally stumbled back inside, chattering and laughing with the excitement of it all. Once downstairs, they went outside. Penelope was reluctant to leave and had a feeling her friends were, too.

"You need to stake your claim to this place," Emma told Fee. "You can't just walk away from it if James decides he wants it."

"What happened to taking control of my life, even if it means leaving the castle?" Fee joked.

"I've changed my mind. You could do so much with a wonderful property like this one."

Fee just shrugged. "Bethany wanted it to go to James."

"Because she was superstitious," Ava argued. They'd all heard that story. Bethany had thought her daughters had died because her family had messed with the proper lines of inheritance. In reality, they'd simply been in a car accident.

"You should get a lawyer. Bring James to court. Get it figured out," Penelope said.

"The thing is, if I do that, I risk losing the place," Fee said. "As long as I keep quiet and James doesn't stake his claim, I get to stay."

"I understand that now," Emma assured her. "I hope you figure things out, though, so you can have the life you deserve."

"I hope so, too," Fee said.

WES BREATHED A sigh of relief when Penelope left the house and Amber went outside to talk to her renovation team. Now he could get down to business. He crossed the room and tapped Olivia on the shoulder.

"You think this is right?" he asked when she turned to face him. "Destroying someone's home like this?"

"Like I told you two before, this is what we do," she said irritably. "People love it when I put my mark on things. No one's ever been this weird about it."

"Penelope renovated this house by hand. She just spent months getting this room perfect."

Olivia snorted. "You call the decor in here perfect? Come on—it was trite. It was done. It was so boring it was bored of itself."

"That's rich, coming from you."

Olivia blinked at him. "Are you saying I'm—"

"You're bored. With all of this. That's clear, so why don't you do something different? Something productive for once? You know, anyone can destroy something. Only truly creative people can build something new."

"I am building something new. I'm a presence. I'm a breath of fresh air. I come in and liven things up. This"—she waved a hand—"this is the absence of presence."

"Are you even listening to yourself?" Wes knew he

had to keep his head. "Do you even love the guy you're marrying? Because usually a bride is focused on her groom the week before her wedding, not on trashing the venue where she's holding the ceremony."

Something flickered in Olivia's eyes, and Wes knew he'd hit the mark. Olivia couldn't be more than twenty. She was nervous about this wedding. About her future. Was that why she was lashing out?

"You don't have to go through with it, you know." He dropped his voice. "Give me the word, and I'll help you get out of it."

"I don't want out of it!" Her eyes went wide. "Why would you say that?"

"What's going on here?" Amber, coming back in, hurried to intervene.

"Nothing," Wes said. "There's absolutely nothing important happening here at all."

There it was—that flare of Olivia's eyelids again. The one that told him she cared what he thought of her. Wanted him—and everyone else—to be impressed with her. He had a chance here he wasn't going to get again. Wes decided to take it.

"Where do you belong?" he challenged her. "Where's home to you?"

"Home?" Olivia blinked at him. "I… I mean…"

"Olivia has homes in Los Angeles, New York and London," Amber said stoutly.

"I'm not talking about houses. I'm talking about the

one place you feel safe and loved." Wes didn't know how he knew this was the right question to ask, except that something in Olivia reminded him of... himself. It was an uncomfortable thought. One he didn't have time to pursue just now.

Olivia shrugged, but she couldn't quite pull it off. "I'm home wherever I am. Wherever my people are."

"The people you have to pay to hang out with you?" He was pushing his luck. Amber scowled, but before she could intervene, he went on. "Olivia, there's so much more to life than that. Marrying someone should be the first step to creating a real home."

"How would you know?" The venom in her voice told him this conversation was over. All he could hope was she'd heard something of what he'd said. She was young and rich and pretty and didn't deserve his pity, but she struck him as a woman careening down a steep slope, about to sail right off the edge into the abyss. Maybe she did love Vincent, but the life she was living was all for the cameras. You couldn't build a long-term relationship on a foundation that shaky.

"You shouldn't be using her like this," he said to Amber. "You ought to be steering her into a career and lifestyle she can sustain for years. Are you just going to drop her when her brand crashes and burns? Because this"—he waved a hand to encompass the destruction they'd wrought together—"isn't the kind of thing that lasts."

"What does he mean?" Olivia asked Amber.

"Nothing," Amber said firmly. "He's just a no one who doesn't know anything."

"Where are her parents?" Wes pressed.

"My parents?" Olivia's voice rose in a way that was becoming all too familiar. "My parents never gave a damn until I started making money. Now they want their share. Well, screw that."

So he was right. Olivia had never had a real home, either.

"You see what you've done? You've upset her. Come on, Olivia." Amber put an arm around Olivia's shoulders and drew her away from him. "Let's talk about how to arrange the deck."

"I hate this place," Olivia said as they walked away. "I hate everything."

"By the time I'm done with it, you'll love it," Amber assured her.

By the time Amber was done with it, Wes wasn't sure there'd be anything left.

His phone buzzed in his pocket. He pulled it out, heading upstairs to Penelope's apartment, when he saw it was his father.

"What?" he said when he answered.

"You know what. Where are you?"

"I'm in California."

"You said you'd be back here by the end of the day."

Wes stifled a growl. "No, you said you wanted me

back today. I told you I'll be home on Sunday, and that's when you'll see me. I don't have time for this." He hung up, but he knew he couldn't run away from his parents forever.

CHAPTER 7

"*Y*OU'RE SAVING MY sanity, you know," Wes said when they were on the water the following morning. The sky was streaked with pink and orange clouds, the sun just edging up over the horizon. They'd had a quick breakfast at Sunnyside Diner. Penelope had tried to pay since she'd lost the competition yesterday, but Wes insisted on covering the bill.

"You're saving mine." Penelope didn't think she'd have survived the last few days without these hours on the boat. All the rhythms of taking it out, fishing, bringing it home and stowing the gear away were soothing to her soul, while every moment she spent in Olivia Raquette's company grated like nails on a chalkboard. At least nothing more had been destroyed at her home during her hours away yesterday. She should probably thank Wes for that, too.

Her tour of the castle had been a good distraction. She'd spent the drive to the marina earlier trying to explain to Wes what it was like.

"We could keep going, you know," he said now.

"Just disappear down the coast. Live on fish and sunshine."

"Sounds wonderful," Penelope admitted. "Are you really going to give up your plan to be a fishing guide and be CEO of your parents' company?"

"Don't see how I'm going to get out of it." Wes tested the pull of his line, but it was clear no fish had taken his bait.

"Don't your parents want you to be happy?"

"Not really. They've always had certain expectations for their kids."

"That's harsh."

"What about your parents? Didn't they ever have expectations of you?"

Penelope fell silent. The truth was they hadn't, really. She supposed they had a somewhat old-fashioned take on things. Her mom had always been a housewife. Penelope did well in school and attended San Jose State, but no one had pushed her to set goals—or helped her dream big. She didn't think they'd have stood in her way if she'd wanted a career, but she'd always worked for Uncle Dan and thought she always would.

"Not really," she said finally and busied herself with her fishing rod.

"You're lucky."

Maybe, Penelope thought, or maybe it meant her parents didn't think she'd amount to much.

That wasn't true, she told herself. Her parents had

honored her love for the *Amphitrite* and the time she got to spend with Uncle Dan. They'd sent her to school so she'd have a fallback plan, but otherwise they'd kept their thoughts to themselves and supported her desire to work with him.

"It would be different if my sister hadn't lost her mind," Wes said after they'd sat silent for some minutes. "She was embezzling money."

"She told you that?"

"Not exactly," he admitted. "She said that's what Mom and Dad accused her of, and then she tried to defend herself. I shut that down."

Penelope was quiet a moment. "What if she didn't do it?"

"Mom and Dad wouldn't make up something like that. No wonder they're so devastated. They trusted her."

"Do they run the company or does she?"

Wes could understand her confusion. "About five years ago, my parents stepped back from the day-to-day operations. Mom and Dad still have their fingers in all the pies, though."

"How did she get away with it, then?"

"She didn't," he said. "I've barely talked to them, but I'm getting the feeling they want to keep it hush-hush. They'll install me as CEO, at least until it all dies down. Maybe in a few years I can hand operations back to them."

"Will they want to come out of retirement?"

"Maybe." The truth was he didn't know what they wanted or why they'd stepped back in the first place. Could you come out of retirement when you'd never really retired at all? They were still young and still rabid about keeping control over decisions when it came to their company.

"Sounds like you have a lot to talk to them about."

"I've been putting that off." He got a tug on his line and started reeling in the fish.

"You'll feel better when you know all the details," Penelope told Wes when they'd popped the lingcod into the well.

"All the details of what?"

"Whatever is going on with your folks. They need to know you want to try your hand at guiding again."

He snorted. "That'll go over well. Besides, what about you? You don't want to be a wedding-venue host. You want to spend your days on the water. Anyone can see that. Why aren't you gunning for the future you want?"

"That's different."

"Is it? How?"

"I feel guilty I even have the *Amphitrite*. I told you— Uncle Dan didn't get a chance to change his will. If he had, one of my cousins would probably own it."

"He's gone, right? You can't know what he really wanted. The boat went to you, and it's obvious you're a natural at the job."

"Am I?"

"Don't you think you are?" he countered.

"I do," she said dispiritedly, "but there are other considerations. Let's face it, most fishing parties are made up of men. Would they even want a female guide?"

"Why not?"

She gave him a look.

"Tailor your business to women, then."

"There wouldn't be enough all-female parties to make a living off."

"Then do both. A skilled guide will get enough business over time."

"And when I take a group of men out and they start drinking? I'm strong and I'm smart, but at the end of the day…" She let her words trail off.

"At the end of the day, a group of drunk men is a group of drunk men," he finished for her. Wes surveyed her. "Could you hire a cousin or something? Someone you absolutely trusted?"

"Do you know how angry it makes me that I even need to think about that?" As soon as she said the words out loud, she realized they were true. She was angry, and she'd been angry for a long time. Ever since Roger had…

Penelope pushed the memory out of her mind, but the anger remained. She was having a hard time letting it go these days.

He nodded. "I get that, but honestly, if I was bringing a potentially rowdy party out on the ocean, I'd make sure I had one or two other guys around. Hiring help doesn't mean you're not capable. It just means you're being realistic."

"I feel like I'd lose control." She swallowed against the pain of that thought. She wanted to trust her cousins, but they were typical guys. They'd want to be in charge sooner or later.

"In what way?" Wes asked. He deftly re-baited her line, readied the reel and handed it back to her, giving her time to get her emotions under control. She appreciated the small courtesy even as part of her wanted to say she could have done it herself.

"You know what would happen if I hired my cousin Alex to work on the *Amphitrite*? The first party of men that came aboard would look to him for everything. When they needed equipment, they'd ask him for it. If they wanted to know what bait to use, they'd go to him for advice. Needed help reeling in a fish? They'd call Alex. I'd disappear into the woodwork."

"You might have to assert yourself, but you wouldn't disappear unless you wanted to, and if Cousin Alex started acting like the owner of the boat, you'd fire his ass."

Penelope smiled at that. Damn straight she would. "Okay, so what you're really saying is I'm being over-dramatic."

"I'm saying you're letting your fears get in the way of the future you really want."

"So are you," she said. "You think your parents will be furious if you don't take that job."

"They won't just be furious. They'll cut me out of the family for good."

WES WISHED HE could take the words back the moment he'd said them. Penelope, about to cast her line, stopped and faced him.

"You think they'll disown you if you don't go and work for them?"

"I know they will. They barely keep me around as it is. The only reason they want me now is because Grace messed up so badly."

"Wes."

He didn't want her pity. "I was never the son they wanted. They already had to pay the bills for my food, housing and education growing up."

"You mean the things parents pay for when they have children?" Penelope broke in. "That's not some sacrifice they made, Wes. That's what they signed on for when they gave birth to you."

"They've paid me a salary since I left school, even though I barely work for them."

Penelope's brows pushed together. "Why would they do that?"

"Because your first-born son is supposed to step into

your shoes. He's supposed to work his way up in your company and take over for you someday. They felt like they had to give me a position in the company, even if my lack of aptitude for it made it easier for all of us if I stayed away most of the time."

"I don't understand any of what you're saying," Penelope told him. "No way my dad—or uncle—would have paid me a dime if I didn't do a full day's work."

"I'm not cut out for the business."

"If I'd been a lousy fisherman, Uncle Daniel would have sent me packing. He'd have told me to be a lawyer or a nurse or whatever I did qualify for. Why didn't you get some other job?"

"What if I messed it up? My parents wouldn't be able to cover for me. Their friends would know what a dud I was."

"Why would they care? What kind of people are your parents hanging out with?"

"Their clients. Other successful businesspeople whose children aren't complete failures."

Penelope stared at him. "You think you're a failure?"

"By their standards." Her reaction was making him feel worse. "I know what I'm good at. This." He swept a hand through the air to indicate the boat, the rods and the fish. "I'm fine with who I am, but they're not. They wanted something different. Can you blame them? It's hard to brag about your son the fisherman."

"I don't see why not if you work hard and you're

good at what you do. My parents wouldn't have cared what job I chose as long as I showed up, did my best and was dependable. They definitely wouldn't have disowned me for following my own inclinations."

"Are you kidding? You're terrified your uncle Dan is going to come back from the dead and flay you alive for taking out the *Amphitrite*."

Penelope pulled back. Thought that over. "You're right," she said ruefully. "I am. God, we're a pair, aren't we?" She set her rod in one of the holders. "It isn't right. Parents are supposed to love their children unconditionally. So are uncles. If they can't, we need to find that comfort somewhere else."

"Like where?" He expected her to say something about finding his soul mate or to wait until he had children of his own. Penelope stayed silent for a long time.

"I think maybe we need to find it within ourselves," she said finally.

Wes swallowed a sudden rise of pain in his throat. "I can't be my own family," he said gruffly.

"That's what I'm doing these days." Penelope turned back to fishing. They didn't talk for a long while. When they did they stuck to safe topics like the way the wind was picking up and whether or not they would get any more bites.

Wes made sure they packed up and headed in on time. He was determined Penelope's business wouldn't be harmed in any way by his presence at Fisherman's Point this week. EdgeCliff Manor, he corrected himself sourly. Usually Pen worked swiftly when it was time to stow their fishing gear away and ready the boat for the return trip, but today she slowed down, lost in thought more than once.

"You okay?" he asked the next time they passed each other.

"Tired," she admitted. "I'm not getting much sleep these nights."

"I hear that." It was Penelope keeping him up at night, though. Was it worry keeping her awake?"

Without thinking, he reached for her and folded her into his arms. Penelope rested against his chest without protest, letting out a shuddering breath and relaxing against him. There was nothing sexual about their embrace, but Wes felt a surge of attraction just the same. He wished he could be the person who made Penelope's day better. That he could be her family and she could be his.

When she tilted her chin up to face him, it was only natural to bend down to kiss her. Penelope felt so right in his arms. It was as if he'd known her for years, not days. Her hair smelled lemony, her curls were soft and warm where they brushed his face. She kissed him back willingly, and the connection between them soon had all his senses firing up to full awareness.

"We'd better go," she said softly when they parted.

He didn't protest, even though he wanted to. Instead, he found reasons to touch her on their way home, each press of his fingers against her skin reminding him of what he really wanted to do with her.

They didn't see Mac today, but when they arrived home, it was clear some new event was occurring at the house. A huge limousine was parked half in the driveway, half in the street, causing a bottleneck on Cliff Street.

"For heaven's sake," Penelope said. She kept driving, parked down the road and hurried back to the house. By the time they made it there, the limousine was backing out, inch by inch, to the blare of car horns.

Penelope didn't stop to watch. She opened the door to the house and marched inside, Wes following close behind.

"Vincent is here," Amber said in a clipped voice, making a beeline across the great room to meet them. "Watch yourself."

"Watch myself?" Penelope parroted. "Is he violent?"

"He's a star. They're all unstable," Amber said, as if they should know this already. "Be on your toes, do as you're told and keep a low profile. Ah," she added, looking behind them. Wes turned to see the door to the street had opened again, letting in a man carrying an enormous speaker. "The sound system is here, too."

Wes caught Penelope before she could react and pulled her into the great room, now barren of all furniture and stripped of kitchen cabinets and appliances, too, before she was run over by the string of men who followed the first one into the hall behind them.

"We can't have that kind of sound system here," she protested as they watched the workers carry speaker after speaker into the room. "There's a noise ordinance."

"We'll take it up with Amber." He could see this crew of men wasn't going to listen to anything they said. One by one they dropped the large black speakers. Penelope winced with every thud.

"Where do we set up?" the first man asked.

"Over there." Amber pointed to the far corner.

Wes grabbed Amber's arm as she walked away. "We need to talk to you."

"What is it now?" Amber's annoyance was clear.

"There's a noise ordinance in this neighborhood. That sound system isn't going to fly," Penelope said. "Neither is the number of guests you told me."

"Well, that's too bad, because the number of guests has gone up. We're at one hundred and twenty. We'll need more seating. And a bigger deck."

"You can't have either," Penelope said. "And you definitely can't turn on that sound system."

"Fine—we'll run the music through smaller speakers. People will think it's loud because they'll see the big ones," Amber said. "Smoke and mirrors—that's what we do." She pulled away from Wes's grip and kept going.

"Oh, here you are," Olivia said, appearing from the

direction of the stairs, a fresh-faced, muscle-bound blond manchild in tow. "This is Vincent. My intended."

"Nice to meet you," Wes hurried to say when Penelope opened her mouth but didn't manage to find any words. He knew why she was struggling: Vincent looked all of twelve, despite the muscles. Were they really supposed to be afraid of this guy?

"Y-yes, nice to meet you," Penelope managed. "Did you have a good trip?"

"Whatever. Where's the game room?"

"Uh… we don't have one."

"Babe, I don't have time for this. I've got to practice!" Vincent turned on Olivia.

"He's one of the best at Road Invasion," Olivia announced proudly. "Amber's got a setup for you somewhere," she told Vincent. "Hold on. Amber!" she hollered. Amber came running. "Where's the game room?"

"Up the stairs, take a right, two doors down," Amber rattled off. "Snacks and drinks in the refrigerator."

"There's no refrigerator in that room," Penelope protested.

"There is now."

"I'm going to call you," Penelope called softly to Emma and Ava when she caught sight of them from her balcony that evening. As far as she knew, Olivia and Vincent were still ensconced in the second-story game room, but Amber was down on the first-floor deck and she didn't want to be overheard.

Back inside, when she got them on the line, she brought them up to date on Vincent's arrival and the enormous sound system.

"I can't believe they've been playing video games all day," Ava said. "They have the beach, the redwoods…"

"If it isn't on a screen, it's not real to them," Penelope said. "Or maybe it's a form of pre-wedding jitters."

"And shooting imaginary enemies with imaginary guns is soothing them?" Ava asked.

"Guess so."

"Any more damage to your house?" Emma asked.

"No—but what if the wedding gets so loud and rowdy someone calls the cops? I could get shut down. None of this will be worth it."

"We won't turn you in," Ava assured her. "I don't have any guests the night of the wedding."

"I do," Emma said. "But we're two doors down, and I'll tell them up-front that a very famous, very private wedding is happening."

"Maybe I can get your guests invited," Penelope said worriedly. "Or maybe we should find reservations for them somewhere else on my dime."

"I'll take care of it," Emma promised her.

"What about your handsome fisherman?" Ava asked.

"Wes has been great."

"We need more details than that," Ava pressed.

"We've… kissed a few times," Penelope admitted. "I really like him—and he's going home in a few days."

"That's what Ava kept saying about Sam," Emma reminded her. "And he never actually did go home."

"Wes has to. His parents are depending on him for help. Something happened with his sister, who held an important role in their company, and now they expect him to take her place."

"Does he want to?" Emma asked.

"No. He's doing it out of guilt. And maybe to finally get some approval from them." He hadn't put it in exactly those words, but it was clear to her that's what was happening.

"Don't give up hope," Ava said.

"I don't have any hope to give up."

"Before you go, we have something for you," Emma said. "Maybe it will make you feel better."

A clothesline was strung between Penelope's and Ava's houses, which they used to send things back and forth to each other. There was a similar one between Ava's and Emma's houses. When Penelope stepped out on the deck, she saw Ava tying an enormous bag next to the regular cloth one that hung from the line. When she'd made sure it was secure, Ava sent it across to Penelope.

Penelope bent over the edge of her balcony, making sure to catch the bag before it hit the house. She maneuvered it up and over the railing and struggled to untie it.

Inside, carefully wrapped in paper, was a painting. Penelope recognized the style at once—it was by her favorite local artist.

"Oh, my goodness. Thank you!" It depicted a fishing boat getting underway as sunrise flooded the sky and ocean with color. "I love it," she told them.

"We couldn't replace the one Olivia destroyed, since they're all one-of-a-kind," Ava said, "but we hoped this would make the idea of putting everything back together once she's gone a little less daunting."

"Thank you. It's beautiful." Penelope knew it would always remind her of her early morning fishing excursions with Wes.

"Hang in there," Emma said. "Let us know if there's any way we can help."

"You already have."

Penelope was smiling when she got off her phone. She placed the painting on top of a side table that sat against one wall in her living room area. She'd find a permanent place to hang it after Olivia and her entourage left town. For now she'd keep it safe—and to herself—up here.

Now she only had to get through the four days until the wedding. Her house, which had been perfectly ready to host a small, intimate gathering when Olivia arrived, now looked like a disaster, and she was far from sure the wedding would even happen at all. Penelope found herself wondering again if this could be a publicity stunt designed to boost the careers of a pair of struggling half stars.

The thought of the wedding not happening at all was worse than the thought of it going ahead—and flopping. What if all this turned out to be a great big joke?

"How about a beer?" Wes said, coming into the room. He'd been holed up in his bedroom, where he'd gone to take a call from his parents.

"Sure," Penelope said glumly. She doubted alcohol would still her whirling thoughts, but it was worth a try. "How are your folks?"

"Impatient. They want me home. My mom was grilling me on how many fish I'd caught. I think she thought she could shame me into cutting my trip short if I'd already got a bunch."

"Which you have." They were processed and stored in the chest freezer in her shed. She'd send them to New Jersey for him when his trip was over.

"She doesn't know that. I'm afraid she's not going to think too highly of your guiding skills. Anyway, I'm going to hit the ground running next week. My folks have set up an intensive training program for me. Guaranteed to make me a high-powered executive in six months."

"Sounds exciting."

"Sounds like hell." Wes handed her a beer and led the way onto the deck. He sat down heavily on one of the wrought-iron chairs. "What am I doing?"

"You're trying to be a good son."

"I wish I was a selfish bastard."

Penelope laughed. "Oh yeah? What would you do if you were?"

"I'd start by scooping you up, hauling you off to my room and making love to you. Then maybe I could think straight."

Penelope stilled, her bottle of beer halfway to her mouth. She set it down on the table with a thump as she pictured an encounter like that. Lust spiked through her, along with a desire to flip off the world—especially Olivia and Vincent. Why should a pair of surly just-past-teenagers get to have all the fun?

"Why don't you?" she finally asked.

Wes nearly choked before he managed to swallow the mouthful of beer he'd just swigged. "Are you serious?"

"Why not? I've been trying to be sensible, starting a stupid wedding business, but the way this week is going, why shouldn't I say to hell with it and sleep with you?"

"I'm not sure those are the best reasons, but I like your conclusion." Wes sat forward in his chair. "I need you to be sure you want this, though," he said. "Fishing buddies aren't easy to come by, after all."

"Oh, shut up," Penelope said. "I'll still let you bait my hook in the morning, if that's what you're asking."

"That's what I'm asking."

"Well, I will. I'll take you fishing, Wes Abbott, even if it turns out you're a lousy lay."

"No one said anything about that," he sputtered as he stood up. She'd only half risen herself when he ducked down, tossed her over his shoulder and lurched for the door into the apartment.

"Don't strain your back," she called.

"I'm not straining my back. What the hell, woman? This is supposed to be romantic."

"It's actually kind of uncomfortable," she said when they'd made it through the living room. She began to wriggle, and Wes staggered, crashing against the wall.

"Shhh," Penelope said.

"Shh, yourself." He made it to the door to his room, ducked a little to make sure she didn't hit the header and tossed her on the bed. He shut the door behind them and quickly stripped down.

"Oh, that's nice." Penelope shifted over, making room for him.

"You're overdressed," he told her when he joined her.

"You could help me with that."

Help her he did. First out of the T-shirt that was hugging her curves, then out of her jeans. He sat back to get a good look at the way her surprisingly lacy bra cradled her breasts. When he reached for her, Penelope came happily into his embrace, and together they got rid of the rest of the clothing between them.

"Why did we wait so long to do this?" Penelope murmured a few minutes later, when they'd had time to explore each other's bodies.

"I don't know. I'm glad we're not waiting anymore," Wes said.

THIS WAS HIS idea of paradise, Wes thought the following morning when Penelope was still sleeping, naked, beside him, her luxurious curls tickling his shoulder. He loved this bed. As far as he could tell, there wasn't anything special about it, but it had to be the best bed he'd ever slept in. He loved this room, too. The cozy nest Penelope had created just for people like him. He'd give anything to stay right here with her and forget the rest of the world. He'd half expected to be interrupted last night by their guests, but no one had knocked on their door; they'd been able to lie tangled together, dreaming of leaving it all behind for a life onboard the *Amphitrite*.

When Penelope's eyes opened, he dropped a kiss on her head. "Morning."

"Good morning." She stretched, and the sheet that covered her slipped down to remind him of the way her body had felt so damn good joined with his last night.

She reached for her phone, checked the time and groaned. "We've got to get up if we're going to have time to fish."

Wes was torn between wanting another morning on

the ocean with her and staying right here.

"Come on, sailor, get going," she said, reading his mind. "We can fool around tonight in the dark. We won't be able to fish then."

"Okay, okay," he grumbled, getting up.

As they moved through the apartment like an old married couple, getting dressed, taking turns in the bathroom, packing the necessary items for a morning on the boat, Wes realized he'd never felt so comfortable with anyone before. He wasn't worried that Penelope would feel like he was taking up too much space or intruding where he wasn't wanted. Penelope wasn't constantly hovering, telling him to watch some expensive piece of art or keep his voice down or suggest that maybe he cut his visit short, the way his folks always seemed to.

He'd experienced hospitality before, of course, but usually he was paying for the privilege.

Which he was now, he reminded himself. He was Penelope's paying customer.

That wasn't all he was to her, though. She'd shared her body with him freely last night, but it was more than that. She had shared her thoughts, hopes and dreams with him, too.

Wes stopped looking for his sunglasses and stood still in the middle of the living room.

"What's wrong?" Penelope asked.

"You're going to marry someday. Have kids." He

wasn't sure if he was asking a question.

"Yes," Penelope said. "That's what I want."

That was what he wanted, too. With someone like Penelope, Wes realized. He wanted a guiding business. A home. A wife. A family. Penelope wanted a life like that.

He wasn't going to be able to find out if they could have it together, though. Her life was here, in California. She already had the home. The boat. The business.

All he had was a nightmare waiting for him in New Jersey.

CHAPTER 8

A FEW HOURS of fishing would bring her to rights, Penelope told herself. Spending the night with Wes was wonderful, but waking up to reality proved to be harder than she expected. One night with him wasn't enough, and it didn't help that he'd started asking questions about her future plans.

The truth was, she'd always pictured herself with children, even if that vision did clash with the idea of spending most of her days on the *Amphitrite*. In the past she'd had a shadowy idea that her mother might step in to spend grandmotherly days with the children when Penelope was on the boat.

She supposed that wasn't fair to her mother, who was still a young woman with plans and dreams of her own. Now that she lived in Costa Rica, none of it mattered. Penelope didn't have any sisters or close female cousins who weren't working full-time themselves. She knew the cost of childcare—it was as prohibitive as the price of a home was around here.

"We should get going," she said to Wes.

"I'm ready."

As usual, they opened and closed the door to her apartment with exaggerated care and crept down the stairs so as not to wake any guests, but when they reached the ground floor, Penelope realized with a sinking heart there'd be no fishing today.

A light was on in the great room. Olivia was sitting cross-legged on the floor, a box of donuts next to her. As Penelope tiptoed into the room, Olivia tried to hide the pastry she was eating, then gave up and flourished it defiantly.

"So I'm eating, so what?" she asked.

"I'm glad you're eating. I'm a firm believer in food." Penelope wondered who had fetched it for her and if Amber would fire that person when she found out. "But it's awfully late—or early, as the case may be. Why aren't you sleeping?"

"Why aren't I sleeping?" Olivia parroted in a sing-song voice. "Because my fiancé has been playing Road Invasion for the past eighteen hours."

"That sounds boring," Penelope said sympathetically.

"It's messed up!" Olivia exploded. "He's supposed to be paying attention to me! We're getting married in three days."

Penelope sighed. This problem wasn't going to go away in a matter of minutes. When Olivia wasn't looking, she shrugged and raised her eyebrows. Wes got the point.

"I'll give you ladies a few minutes," he said optimistically, but two hours later Penelope was still sitting on the floor listening to a diatribe that got more and more pathetic.

"The last time we were skateboarding, he kept doing tricks and showing me up. There were these girls there and—"

"Fresh air, that's what we need," Penelope announced. It was getting light out, and they definitely weren't going fishing. "Come on," she said to Wes, who'd been in and out of the room several times to see if there was any chance of her getting away. "Let's go for a walk."

"I don't want to go for a walk," Olivia whined.

Penelope didn't bother to answer. She hauled the young woman to her feet and marched her outside, stopping only to find some shoes for both of them. Wes shadowed them as she led the way down the street and into the Cliff Garden. They wound along the paths to a bench that looked over the Pacific Ocean.

"Let's watch the sunrise." She pulled Olivia down beside her.

Wes continued to prowl the paths. A few minutes later Emma joined them, as Penelope knew she would. Emma was in charge of the Trouble Bench, as she called this seat, a tradition she'd inherited from her grandmother. She could see the bench from her house. Whenever a lost soul found his or her way there, she came to tend them. Often she brought food, but today she carried a steaming mug in her hand.

"I brought you cocoa." She handed it to Olivia, who duly took a sip without question. Penelope realized Olivia was so used to being waited on it didn't strike her as odd that a strange woman would serve her on a garden bench.

Emma sat beside her. "Tell me about it," she said.

"He's such a selfish jerk," Olivia started and in moments was pouring out her tale of woe about Vincent all over again. Penelope breathed a sigh of relief. Emma was so much better at this than her.

By the time Ava came along for their traditional morning walk, Olivia was in a much better mood. Emma suggested that she and Penelope join them.

"Some activity would do you good, don't you think?" Emma asked her. "Sometimes it's easy to overthink things that aren't really problems at all."

"I guess," Olivia agreed.

Penelope got up, found Wes and filled him in on the new plan. When they returned to the bench, Emma was talking on her phone. She cut the call. "Noah and Sam are coming. They're going to take Wes surfing if he wants to go."

"Sure. That sounds great." Wes brightened up. "Do you mind?" he asked Penelope.

"Not at all. I was supposed to have asked them to take you days ago and forgot all about it, didn't I? I'm sorry."

"Don't be. I've had a fantastic week."

"We'll meet up later, when you're back."

"Yeah, we will." He lowered his voice, making it sound suggestive. When he headed off with the other men, Ava gave her an appraising look.

"Things going well with the fisherman?"

"He's Penelope's assistant," Olivia asserted.

"That's right. A very competent assistant," Penelope said, exchanging a smile over Olivia's head with her friends.

While Emma kept chattering with Olivia, peppering her with questions about her career and her plans, and offering suggestions for compromises around how much time Vincent spent gaming, Penelope fell back with Ava.

"I'm totally hooked," she said. "Wes and I were together last night, and it was fabulous."

"Maybe he'll stay?" Ava ventured.

"Or maybe I'm about to get my heart torn to shreds."

"YOU DID PRETTY good for your first time," Sam said. Ava's husband had dark hair, dark eyes and tan skin. He was far from an expert himself, but he had a head start on Wes—he'd been surfing for a month or so. Noah was the real expert. He rode the waves with panache, and when he'd had enough, he took out his camera and photographed other surfers.

Today he'd focused on getting Wes to stand up long enough to ride a wave, which Wes had done in the end a couple of times, although not too gracefully.

"Do you get out here often?" he asked the others as they were paddling in.

"Almost every day."

"Since we both work for ourselves, we can be flexible," Noah said. "It's a hell of a life."

Wes wished he could have that life. Fishing in the morning, surfing in the afternoon—what else could he want except Penelope by his side? It was far too early to have thoughts like that about a woman he'd just met, yet here he was—having them.

Surfing had kept his brain occupied for the last few hours, but now images of Penelope from last night began to fill his mind. She'd been wonderful in his arms. They'd caught each other's rhythms instantly, and that comfort extended well beyond the bedroom. He had no doubt he could make a life with her—if he had the chance.

Winston, Noah's golden retriever, came bounding up to them the moment they emerged onto the sand. He'd waited patiently for them while they were in the water, but the way his tail was wagging told Wes he was happy they'd rejoined him on land.

They met up with two other men whom Noah and Sam had introduced Wes to at the beginning of the day. Greg and Reese belonged to the Surf Dads. Together with their wives—the Surf Moms—they helped each other with childcare and other responsibilities so they could still get out on the waves despite their growing families.

Like Noah and Sam, Greg and Reese apparently had the kind of professional lives that allowed them the flexibility to spend a Wednesday morning surfing.

Wes wouldn't have anywhere near that level of flexibility after this week.

"You're quiet all of a sudden," Greg observed.

"Discouraged?" Reese suggested. "People expect way too much their first time surfing. You did better than most, believe me."

"It's not that. I'm just wondering if there will ever be a second time."

Noah and Sam nodded sympathetically.

"It took me a long time to arrange my life so I could live the way I wanted," Noah said. "It's all worth it in the end, though."

"Sometimes it doesn't take as long as you think it might," Sam put in. "You just have to order your priorities right."

Wes considered that for a minute. "Doesn't family always come first?" he asked with a sigh.

"In my book it does," Noah said, but Wes knew he was thinking of Emma and the baby that was on the way. Wes was thinking of his parents' expectations and the way they were squeezing all the possibilities out of his life.

He helped haul the surfboards up the bluffs to No-ah's and Sam's houses. On his way to Fisherman's Point—EdgeCliff Manor, he corrected himself with an inner groan—his phone buzzed.

Grace again.

"What now?" he asked when he accepted the call.

"You need to get home to New Jersey. Take the CEO job just like Mom and Dad want you to. As soon as you're in, you need to meet with me. I—"

"Meet with you? Why would I do that? You embez-zled money from the company."

"No, I didn't. I swear, Wes. You know I wouldn't do anything like that. I keep trying to tell you."

"How would I know that? I don't know you at all."

There was a long pause on the other end of the line. "Is that what this is all about? You're mad that I've always been Mom and Dad's favorite? Is that why you're jumping to do their dirty work?"

"I'm not jumping to do anything. I don't want to be CEO. I don't want to work for them! You're the one forcing my hand. Do you know what you're doing to my life?"

Grace hesitated again. "Hell. You know what? You're right, Wes. I'm sorry. You don't know me at all. I could blame Mom and Dad for that, but the truth is it's just as much my fault. When we were kids, I saw how they treated you, and it scared me to death. The more they yelled at you, the more perfect I tried to be. The more you got in trouble, the more I pushed you away. When they sent you to school, I thought my turn was next. I shut everything down except making sure that wouldn't be the case."

"You did a good job."

"Yeah. A great job." She sounded bitter. "Mom and Dad learned I'd do whatever they told me, no matter what."

"You can't blame them for the fact you stole the money."

"Really? You think a lifetime of falling into line prepared me to be a criminal? It didn't, Wes. I didn't embezzle anything."

For one moment, Wes hesitated. Then he remembered who he was talking to. Grace was the one who'd always been welcome at his parents' home. The one they'd groomed to take over their precious company. The one who'd ratted him out every time he came home and made the slightest transgression of their rules.

She wasn't the victim here.

"You know what?" he broke in. "I can't listen to this. I've got somewhere to be." He hung up. Grace had made her own bed. It was time for her to sleep in it.

When he got to Fisherman's Point, he saw with a glance that Penelope wasn't downstairs. He climbed up to the third floor, let himself in the apartment with a soft knock and smiled to see her sitting on the deck, her feet propped up on the railing, balancing a plate of breakfast on the arm of the chair. His worry about Grace slid away as he joined her there, leaning down to drop a kiss on the top of her head.

"Glad you're back," she told him. "Go grab some food."

He did so, at ease in the small kitchen. He was happy here, he realized. Penelope's home was everything his parents' had never been.

And he didn't want to leave.

SHE'D KNOWN WES for only a week, Penelope reminded herself the following morning when they pulled in behind EdgeCliff Manor after another spell of fishing. They had the whole operation down to a science, as if Wes had transformed into Uncle Dan and this was merely an extension of her years spent on the *Amphitrite* with him.

Last night they'd made love several times and finally fallen asleep out of sheer exhaustion. She'd woken this morning happy in spite of all her worries. It had been hard to concentrate on fishing, but they'd done their best, snagging kisses in between catches until Penelope wished they could return to bed.

For once her CRV fit in the parking area between the house and the street. There were a couple of work trucks, but no spillover of extra vehicles. Penelope prayed everyone would be safely asleep today. So far

Olivia and Amber had accepted that as her new personal assistant, Wes would be around all the time, but they hadn't caught on that they were spending their mornings on a fishing boat, and Penelope was determined they never would.

Slipping inside as quietly as possible, she and Wes managed to gain the stairs and make it up to her apartment without being seen, even though she distinctly heard voices in the great room.

"So much for sleeping until ten thirty every day," Penelope said dryly when the door was shut behind them. "I thought it was imperative that I be perfectly quiet until then, but they're always up!"

"Maybe the sunshine and sea air are making Olivia more lively," Wes suggested.

"Or maybe she feels the need to keep vigilant, so Vincent doesn't get away."

When she'd showered and changed, Penelope grabbed a snack and brought it onto the balcony, intending to eat before going down to help Olivia and Amber, but as soon as she saw what was happening in the backyard, she let out a shriek, dropped her dish and raced for the stairs.

"What's wrong? What happened?" Wes, just out of the shower, a towel wrapped around his waist, followed her. "Penelope, are you okay?"

She kept going, racing down two flights of stairs and through the house to the back deck. "Stop!" she yelled as soon as she was outside. "Stop it—now!"

She was too late. She came to a halt among a semicircle of workers who were dismantling the outdoor fireplace she'd built with Uncle Dan when she was a girl. It stood in the far corner of the lawn and was one of her favorite things about this house. Penelope covered her mouth with her hands, tears slipping down her cheeks.

"Why did you do that?" She hated crying in front of strangers, but she was past being able to control her anger—and her dismay. She remembered the day her uncle had marked out the outline of the fireplace on the ground and then patiently allowed her to help pour the cement foundation. She'd been ten and so proud to get to work on the project with him.

"It was an eyesore." But Amber didn't sound as belligerent as usual. She sounded alarmed.

"It was built by my uncle. I helped him. That was irreplaceable!" There was that word again, but this time she meant it, because her uncle was dead and there was no way to recapture what they'd built. Penelope scrubbed her cheeks with the back of her hand.

"It was going to be in the photographs," Amber began.

"Screw the photographs. Screw your need to ruin everything!" Penelope advanced on her.

"You'd better back off, missy." Amber stood as straight as possible, trying to use her height to intimidate Penelope, but Penelope wasn't afraid. Not anymore.

Amber had crossed a line.

Olivia and Vincent arrived, pushing their way through the knot of workmen to get a better view.

"Is there going to be a fight?" Vincent said hopefully.

"What's happening?" Olivia asked.

Penelope pointed at Amber. "She's destroying everything important to me."

Olivia took in the stones and smashed concrete. "What was it?"

"An outdoor fireplace. I used to cook hotdogs and hamburgers over the flames after I went fishing with my uncle. At night he'd tell me ghost stories and we'd make s'mores." Was she still crying? Penelope didn't care. She had every right to grieve. "My uncle died last year. I'll never get to do that again."

Olivia's face took on a pinched look, and it was several seconds before Penelope realized she was struggling not to cry, too. "I went to summer camp once," she said. "When I was little. It was for kids who… whose parents couldn't take care of them." Her voice wobbled, and Penelope wondered if her parents couldn't or *wouldn't* bother to take care of Olivia. The younger woman got control of herself. "We sang songs. Went in canoes sometimes. We slept on the beach once. My counselor was really nice. She always had time for me."

The wistfulness in the young woman's voice tugged at Penelope's heartstrings. Was that one of the few times Oliva had experienced kindness?

"I never went to camp," Vincent said. "Too much being outside. Nothing to do all day."

"There was lots to do all day," Olivia contradicted him, "and it was way more fun than watching you play video games."

Vincent scowled. "I thought you liked watching me."

"Sometimes," she said. "But sometimes I wouldn't mind... *doing* something—together."

"Yeah, right. Like you know how to do anything," Vincent said. "You're meant for looking at, babe."

Penelope reared back. Had he really just said that?

Olivia's mouth dropped open. "I'm not for looking at. I'm in a band," she reminded him. "I'm a singer."

He shrugged. "Sure."

"Vincent!" Olivia looked stricken. Penelope couldn't blame her. She wished she could shake some sense into the young man, but given the size of him, that probably wouldn't work.

"Why are you mad? It's true—you're hot."

"That doesn't mean it's all I'm good for. I'm a whole person, Vincent."

"I know," he said defensively.

Penelope scrubbed her cheeks dry with the back of her arm and decided it was time to take control of the situation, before Vincent managed to make Olivia so angry she called off the wedding.

Two spoiled brats who don't know the meaning of the word work. Her uncle's voice rang in her head. If he was around, he'd fix the situation.

Why shouldn't she?

"You"—she pointed to Vincent—"go get a hammer."

"A hammer? What for?"

"Do it!" She pointed at the house where the various workers had been leaving tools all over the place for days. "And you," she said to Olivia, "go get a broom."

"What for?" Olivia echoed Vincent, but she truly seemed curious to know the answer.

"Your workmen didn't crack the foundation, thank goodness," Penelope told her. "They just busted the stone walls. Vincent will clean the old cement off the stones. You and I are going to rebuild this fireplace."

"Need me to find some cement mix?" Wes put in. He'd gotten dressed and joined them. She turned to him gratefully.

"Would you?"

"Of course."

"Thanks." He leaned in a for a kiss, and Penelope went up on tiptoe to meet it before remembering he was supposed to be her assistant. Amber was still watching them. Penelope pulled back quickly. "Later," she mouthed to him. Out loud, she added, "The rest of you can work on something else. No more destroying things until you talk to me first, okay?"

The workmen grumbled but left.

"You can't order Olivia around like that," Amber

said when everyone was gone.

"She wouldn't go along with it if she didn't want to," Penelope said. "She's bored out of her mind, Amber. Why aren't you keeping her occupied? There's a million things to do in Seahaven. Why aren't you off at the beach, at least? And why aren't you giving Vincent some lessons in manners?"

"This wedding is hush-hush. People know it's going to happen, but they don't know where Olivia is staying yet. I'll leak that information at the perfect time. Until then, she has to stay under wraps. As for Vincent, he's a rising star. He gets to do whatever he wants."

"That's a stupid system, but regardless, you should be grateful to me for giving them something to do before they set the house on fire," Penelope said.

"Whatever. Just remember I'm the one giving orders around here. You're just the help."

WES WAS LEAVING the hardware store when his phone vibrated in his pocket. This time it was his father. Lately he'd called multiple times a day, but Wes had ignored him. Might as well deal with him now.

"Where are you?" his father demanded when he answered.

How many times did he have to repeat himself? He did his best to keep his voice even. "I told you I'll be back in New Jersey by dinner on Sunday." Wes crossed the parking lot to his rental car and unlocked it. Next his father would tell him how inconvenient it was he went away at all.

"Hell of a time for a vacation," his dad thundered, right on cue.

"I made the reservations a year ago, Dad. I informed you about it back then. I can't help that you picked a fight with Grace." He knew once he went home he'd have a hell of a time getting away again. Right now he didn't want to think about how it would feel when he boarded a plane on Sunday. He was trying to enjoy the time he did have with Penelope.

"We need you home today."

"Sorry," he said firmly. "I'm not cutting this trip short."

His father waited on the line, obviously hoping Wes would succumb to his silent pressure. Wes stowed the cement mix in the trunk and climbed into the car. Finally, his father spoke up.

"Look, the shareholders are getting anxious. We've got to handle this right now. They need to see you taking a leadership role."

"How about you take a leadership role, Dad? You ran the business for years before Grace came around. What's the problem?"

"The shareholders are worried about the optics."

"It's only three more days." Wes was losing his patience. Wasn't it enough he was coming at all?

"This is a delicate time."

"Look, Dad, I've got to hang up. I'm about to drive home. Call Grace if you need help." They'd chosen her all this time. It wasn't his fault they'd bet on the wrong horse.

"Your sister isn't coming anywhere near Abbott Enterprises ever again. If you talk to her, you tell her that!"

"Why don't you tell her that?"

"Just get your ass home as soon as you can. I helped you out once when you were in a jam. Now it's your turn." His father hung up.

Wes, about to start the car, sat with his hands on the wheel for a solid minute. His father had never lost his temper like that before. And what was with passing messages to Grace through him?

He started the car and drove to the house slowly. By the time he got there, Penelope and Olivia had the fireplace's foundation cleared of grass and dust, and Vincent was hard at work chipping old cement off the rocks with a hammer and chisel. The ones he'd already cleaned sat in a pile nearby.

"I'll teach you how to mix cement," Penelope was telling Olivia as he approached.

"She's not your servant," Amber reminded Penelope, hovering nearby.

"Don't listen to her," Penelope said confidentially to Olivia. "She's just jealous she doesn't get to build a fireplace."

"I know, right? She always has to be the center of attention," Olivia said.

"Tell me where to find a five-gallon bucket," Wes said to Penelope.

"In the shed on the side of the house. Here, I'll help you find it." She marched quickly around the side of the house. He hurried to follow her, glad no one else seemed to want to come along. When he rounded the corner, Penelope threw her arms around him and kissed him on the mouth.

"What was that for?"

"I've finally figured out how to relate to Olivia." She kissed him again. "By putting her to work."

CHAPTER 9

*P*ENELOPE WOKE UP the next morning with Amber's parting words to her from the previous night still in her ears.

"I expect your full attention tomorrow. We have one day to pull this venue together for the wedding, and we have a packed schedule with vendors and workmen coming and going through the day to make the final preparations. Do you understand me? I'm not going to accept anything less than a hundred percent from everyone, including you."

"Of course," Penelope had said, but she was determined to get Wes on the *Amphitrite* this morning. Tomorrow was Olivia's wedding, and she wouldn't dare go out fishing then. Wes was leaving on Sunday.

This could be their last chance.

Penelope's stomach dipped when she thought about Wes going, especially after the hours of tender lovemaking they'd shared the night before. She'd never experienced a connection like this before. Wes's touch set her on fire. The thought of him leaving and never coming back took her breath away, but there was nothing she could do about that now. She silenced the alarm on her phone, nudged Wes awake and got out of bed.

"Is it fishing time?" Wes rumbled from under the blankets.

"Yes, it is."

He sprang out of bed. "Awesome."

Penelope laughed. "You're awesome."

He came around the bed, pulled her into an embrace and kissed the side of her neck. "I'm definitely going to catch the most fish today. I'm going to wear my lucky shirt." He reached into his duffel bag and pulled out a bright red T-shirt.

"You're going to scare the fish away with that," Penelope teased him.

"No way. You'll see."

"Want the shower?"

"Let's shower together. Faster that way."

Of course it wasn't faster, and Penelope worried they were making enough noise to wake the whole house, but she was glowing with satisfaction as they got their stuff together afterward and began tiptoeing down the stairs.

When Wes cupped her bottom and gave her a squeeze, Penelope swatted at him and nearly knocked them both down the steps, but she caught herself, got her bearings and made it the rest of the way down. Turning toward the door, she came to a halt.

Amber blocked her way.

"Going somewhere?" She looked past Penelope to Wes. "I thought you said we had exclusive use of the house. It's in the contract. I'm beginning to wonder what exactly we're paying you for."

"Wes came early so we could get things done," Penelope stammered. She was a lousy liar and was sure Amber could see right through her.

"I think he's living here," Amber said, proving her right.

"I'm providing round the clock assistance to Miss Rider," Wes said.

"Oh, I'm sure you are," Amber said archly. "But like I said, we're supposed to get exclusive use of this house."

"Wes is helping me get…" What the hell could he possibly help her with?

"S'more sticks," Wes said. "From Italy. You saw how proud Olivia was of the fireplace she built with Penelope."

It was true, Penelope thought. Olivia had glowed when they were done. Even Vincent had gotten into it as the fireplace took shape. Penelope had regaled them with stories about her uncle and how much fun it was to cook outside. They'd forgotten they were celebrities and acted like the just-turned-twenty-year-olds they were. Vincent had proved to have a softer side. It turned out Olivia was good at working with cement, and he'd praised the results when the fireplace was done. He'd even gone so far as to admit he'd been wrong earlier. The kiss they'd exchanged afterward was truly romantic.

"You're flying to Italy?" Amber dragged the sentence out, making it sound even more ridiculous than Wes's statement already was.

"Of course not." Wes met scorn with scorn. "We'll buy them in Big Sur. There's a store there that imports them. Your guests will be talking about them for months."

"My guests won't be toasting marshmallows."

"You sure about that? Olivia seemed to think they would last time I talked to her," Wes countered. Penelope hoped she didn't know the fireplace would need lots more time to cure.

Amber couldn't seem to decide if he was lying or not. In the end she waved them on. "If you are one minute past ten thirty getting back, I will expect you to foot the entire bill for this wedding," she said.

"We'll be back by then," Penelope assured her. Tugging Wes along, she pushed past Amber and kept going.

"I THOUGHT WE'D never get out of there," Wes said when they made it to the car and Penelope was pulling out onto Cliff Street.

"You were brilliant. We're going to have to pick up marshmallow roasting sticks on the way home, though."

"We can do that. I just want to be out on the water with you."

"Me, too."

Wes was glad Penelope was driving. He was too pumped up. He'd thought they were goners when they met Amber in the hallway. He knew if Amber had stopped them, he might never have gotten the chance to go out on the *Amphitrite* again.

Would Penelope still be here if he managed to carve out time for another vacation in a few months? More to the point, would she still be single?

He wanted her again so badly he was aching with need.

He wished he could simply stay.

Penelope suddenly swerved to the side of the road and parked. She turned off the car, undid her seat belt, and climbed over the divider and onto his lap.

"What are you doing?" he managed before she covered his mouth with his own. It was obvious what she was doing, he supposed. He kissed her back, wrapping his arms around her.

"Sorry. Couldn't wait a minute longer."

"I'm going crazy wanting you," he told her.

"Me, too. I think I would have died if we hadn't made it out of the house."

"We'd have to have gotten creative if we stayed. We could have ducked into the shed."

"Or done it against the side of the house," Penelope offered.

"Behind the wall of speakers and amplifiers."

Penelope laughed. "Under the deck."

Wes groaned. Each new vision of being with her took root in his mind, visuals and everything, and his body was responding in a way she could surely feel.

Penelope wriggled her hips, rubbing against him, and it nearly did him in. "I don't think I can wait for tonight to be with you again. Every time we're together, I just want you more."

"I know."

She looked around, took in the traffic passing them. Someone honked a horn. "But we can't get it on right here."

"Not unless we want a ticket for indecent exposure," he agreed.

"We'd better get going." She tilted her head to see out the side window. "There's a front moving in." She nodded to clouds on the horizon. "We might get a little wet on the boat."

"A little water never hurt anything."

IT WAS ONE of the hardest things Penelope had ever done to lift herself off him and climb back into her seat. She was desperate to be close to Wes even though they'd made love in the shower only an hour ago. It had felt much too good to grind herself against him, but they were too exposed here. They'd have more privacy on the boat.

At the marina they bumped into Mac again. She

nearly groaned out loud.

"Have you thought about my offer?" he asked her.

"No," she said truthfully. "I'm not selling."

"You know your uncle wouldn't approve of you taking chances like this."

"Whatever." Penelope kept going, picking up speed as she neared the *Amphitrite*'s berth. She was sick of Mac thinking he knew what was best for her. The *Amphitrite* was hers, plain and simple. She wasn't ever giving it up.

Which meant she probably should be at EdgeCliff Manor supervising every detail of the setup for Olivia's wedding, watching her investment and making sure this whole venture paid off.

She was far too gone now to turn around, however. If she didn't get alone with Wes—right now—she wasn't sure she'd survive.

"You better watch yourself," she heard Mac tell Wes when they were on the dock.

"Sure thing, old man." His footsteps sounded behind her as he caught up. Wes took her hand as they got close to the boat, and they rushed the last few yards, practically falling over each other to get on board.

"Hurry," Wes said.

"I'm hurrying," she assured him. She took another look at the horizon, where clouds formed a dull, dark line. Definitely rain.

She didn't care.

"Ready?" Wes said, casting off the rope.

"Ready." As soon as he was on the boat, she maneuvered the *Amphitrite* carefully out of the harbor, obeying the speed limit until they'd cleared it. Then she opened the engines wide.

Time to get where they could be alone.

PENELOPE DIDN'T VENTURE up or down the coast today; she went straight out from the marina until it was far behind her, cut the engine and tugged her T-shirt up and over her head.

"Now you're talking," Wes told her, hurrying to help her out of her clothes. They made short work of his things. When they were standing together, naked under the broad, darkening sky, Wes gathered her close, his fingers tangling in her hair.

A breeze had picked up on the water, a light, fickle thing that did nothing to lift the oppressive feel of the day. He noticed Penelope looking at the clouds to the west. So they'd get wet. It didn't matter. As long as he could have her again.

"You are everything I've ever wanted," he groaned, meeting her mouth with his own. He felt her tense in his arms, but he kept kissing her until she relaxed again, running his hands up and down her body, drinking in her curves, tasting her, loving the feeling of her in his arms.

They made love on top of a towel on the deck. Wes took his time to draw out both their pleasure. He didn't know when he'd get a chance to be with Penelope on the ocean again like this, and he wanted to make the most of it.

When he'd explored every inch of her body, caressing her until neither of them could wait anymore, he joined with her, moving inside her until the building crescendo of their passion broke free, taking both of them with it.

Afterward, he held Penelope in his arms, wanting to savor every last bit of his time with her. As his senses returned, he realized the waves had gotten choppier in the past half hour. That light breeze was steadier, now, too. Penelope shivered. He pushed himself up to a sitting position. "Let's move this inside." He wasn't done with wanting her. Not by a long shot.

Sparing only a minute to make sure they were safely floating far from anyone else, Wes led Penelope down the companionway. The *Amphitrite*'s cabin was tight, but he wasn't looking for space; he wanted to be as close to Penelope as possible. Piled into the forward bed, pillows propped against the wooden walls, they made love to each other all over again.

This time Wes took even longer to explore Penelope's body, coaxing her into a fever-pitch of wanting before making love to her all over again.

Even after they were done, Wes could have stayed there forever, but sooner than he would have liked, Penelope wriggled out of his embrace and sat up. She pulled the covers of the bunk over her and hugged her arms around her knees.

"What's wrong?" Wes sat up, too, concerned.

"I can't believe I just did that—here," she said.

His heart dropped. "What do you mean?" She regretted making love to him? He'd thought she was as into it as he was. Every time they made love, he lost a little more of his heart to her.

"I forgot all about what happened. The only thing I was thinking about was you."

"And that's a problem?"

She blinked. Turned to him. "Sorry, that came out all wrong."

He waited for her explanation. He knew something had happened to her on the *Amphitrite*. Something that had made her uncle terrified to let her aboard. "Why don't you tell me about it."

She shut her eyes. "Do I have to?"

Normally he wouldn't push her, but whatever it was stood between them, and he couldn't bear that. "I think you do."

He was quiet while she pulled her thoughts together, her fingers pleating the comforter, then smoothing away the wrinkles she'd made.

"A couple of years ago, Uncle Dan slipped on deck. He fell on his hip—hard. He got physical therapy, and over time it improved, but the pain never went away. I think it rattled him. Made him face the fact he was getting older. He was the kind of guy who hated needing any kind of help. They gave him pain pills, of course. He refused to take them."

"He never told me what happened, but I noticed he had a bit of a limp last year."

"He always enjoyed a drink," Penelope went on. "I'm sure you noticed that, too. After his accident he hit the bottle more frequently. He drank with friends, with his fishing clients, by himself… He'd stay up late and sleep it off the next morning."

Wes nodded. Daniel Teresi could knock back a lot of booze. "Let me guess. You picked up the slack?" The last time he was out with Dan, a couple of younger guys had been helping out. Family members of some sort.

"That's right. Which I was more than happy to do," she added. "It made me feel accomplished, you know? I'd get up early, make breakfast for the guests, clean up, get the car loaded, drag Dan out of bed and drive everyone to the marina. Dan would pretend to fix something or whatever while I got the *Amphitrite* running and underway. I took care of the clients for most of the morning. Dan would pull himself together by lunch and take over."

"Sounds like it was working for the two of you."

"Pretty much," Penelope said. "Until Roger Atlas showed up."

"Who's Roger Atlas?"

"The kind of asshole you know is going to be trouble the moment he steps aboard your boat. Before then,

215

even."

Wes nodded. He'd had the misfortune of sharing fishing charters with one or two of those. "What happened?"

She hugged her knees closer to her chest. "It was late August. Dan was in bad shape that day. Roger hadn't slept at our place. He'd booked some other, fancier rental in town and met us at the dock. He'd reserved us for the whole day, just for himself—no family or friends along. Dan and I were loading supplies when he showed up. Roger made some comment about the way I was dressed. 'Not my usual type, but you'll do.' Something like that."

"What did Dan do?" Wes couldn't believe her uncle would let that fly.

"He didn't hear it. When I took him aside and said this one is trouble, he just shrugged me off. Said most rich guys were assholes, but their money paid the bills. Fifteen minutes later, he was fast asleep on one of the bench seats."

Wes knew he wasn't going to like the rest of this story.

"Anyway, I went ahead as usual. Cast off, took the wheel and got us out to a good spot. One of the closest ones where I knew we'd be able to catch a few fish and send Roger home happy, without getting too far away from the marina. Dan wasn't in good shape, and the whole situation was making me uneasy."

"I bet." That sounded like a smart plan.

"Roger caught a good-size halibut right off the bat, which helped. He cheered up a bit. Got less snarky. He caught a second one about a half hour later. When he'd landed it and got his line in the water again, I excused myself for a trip to the head."

Wes waited as she gazed out the porthole at the leaden gray skies. It was starting to rain. The wind had picked up even more.

"I didn't hear him follow me down the companion-way. I was in the cabin when he grabbed me by the hair."

"Jesus."

"It all happened so fast." She threw the covers off and got out of bed, still naked, and stalked through the cabin to stand several feet from the companionway stairs. She turned to face Wes, who'd followed her, so that now her back was to the steps. "I was here when he grabbed me." She arched her back as if Roger had grabbed her hair again, then whirled around, her arms swinging out. Her right hand caught on a small fire extinguisher hanging in a bracket on the wall. The canister came free with a loud ripping sound, and Wes realized it was attached with a large patch of Velcro.

Penelope stood crouched, her head bowed, as if Roger's hand was still tangled in her curls, her left hand forward to try to push him away, her right hand rising, lifting the fire extinguisher higher.

She brought it down. Wes could almost picture the

metal canister crashing against the man's skull. He'd never even met Roger Atlas, but he wished it had been his hand that held that canister.

"I hit him over the head as hard as I could," Penelope said. "Pushed him, too. He fell—nearly took me down with him. Tore out some of my hair." She straightened up, looking at the floor as if Roger lay at her feet. "He hit the back of his head on the first tread of the stairs. I must have been screaming—I don't remember that. Uncle Dan came running. He grabbed Roger, hauled him up the stairs and on deck, yelling at me to shut and lock the hatch, which I did." She turned to face Wes. "That was the worst of it. The long trip back to the marina sitting down here—alone. Not knowing if Roger would attack my uncle or what would happen if he did. When it was clear Uncle Dan had things under control, I started thinking about what might have happened if the fire extinguisher was mounted anywhere else. If Roger hadn't hit his head when he'd fallen. What he might have done." She took a moment to collect her thoughts. "Uncle Dan called in the assault. The police were waiting for us at the marina when we got there. They arrested Roger and put him in a squad car. A couple of them came and got me. Took me off the *Amphitrite* and brought me to the station to give my statement. That's the last trip I took on the *Amphitrite* until you and I went out."

"You said your uncle yelled at you when you tried to

come aboard some time later."

"Everyone in my family said I needed a break from the boat. From fishing. That I had to recover from the attack." She shook her head. "Roger wasn't even charged. It was his word against mine, and he said he'd sue my uncle if I pressed charges. The police brokered a deal. He went home and swore never to come back. I never saw him again. My mom and I took our cruise as usual in early October. After that I wanted to get back to work. As far as I was concerned, I *was* recovered. The whole ordeal lasted half a minute. I lost some hair, that's all. It's like they thought I'd be afraid to ever leave my house again."

"You weren't?"

"No. But maybe that's because something's wrong with me. Maybe I don't have enough common sense."

She had to be repeating something someone else had said to her. Wes reached out and took her hand. She let him lead her to the bed. "From what I just saw, you have more common sense than most people. Your first reaction when you met Roger was that he wasn't to be trusted. You told your uncle not to let him on the *Amphitrite*, right?"

She nodded.

"It was your uncle who didn't use common sense. You did what you could to get Roger in a better mood. You kept him busy. Kept him catching fish."

She nodded again. "But I turned my back on him."

"How the hell can you run a fishing charter and never turn your back on a guest?" Wes countered. "When he followed you and grabbed you, you fought back. You found a weapon. You screamed to draw attention to what was happening. You knocked a man bigger than you to the floor. If your uncle hadn't come, you would have run up those stairs and found a way to lock Roger in, wouldn't you?"

"Of course."

"So the only person on that boat who made a mistake was your uncle." He let that sink in. "And that's why he was mad at you. That's why he wouldn't let you on the *Amphitrite*. Don't you see that?"

She was shaking her head. "He thought I'd get hurt again. He thought I'd brought it on myself—because I'm a woman."

"He was mad because he messed up!" Wes countered. "Because he couldn't stop drinking. Because he couldn't trust himself to stay the hell awake. He couldn't let you back on the boat because he couldn't trust himself to keep you safe." Wes fought to get his emotions under control. He realized he was furious with Penelope's uncle for being so hung over he didn't see the signs of danger himself, even after his niece pointed them out, and then for being such a coward that he let her take the blame rather than admitting who was really at fault. "He was ashamed, Penelope. He knew it was his fault, and he couldn't stand it, so he let you think something was wrong with you. There isn't. You're perfect. I love you."

Her lips parted and her eyes went wide.

"I mean it," Wes said. "I love you. You're not to blame for any of this. Roger is the bad guy. Your uncle is the one who made all the mistakes. You're amazing, don't you see that? You don't deserve to lose your dreams because of him."

The boat pitched suddenly, and both of them snapped their heads around to look out the porthole. The cloudy sky had grown downright ominous. The wind was howling around them, and the *Amphitrite* rocked side to side. Rain spattered against the glass.

"Hell," Wes said. "We'd better get back."

"You really think Uncle Dan was angry at himself?" Penelope asked, reaching for her clothes.

"I know it. The *Amphitrite* is yours now, Penelope. You're a fantastic guide. You've got a good head on your shoulders. You're the one who gets to decide what to do next."

CHAPTER 10

*P*ENELOPE DRESSED QUICKLY and made her way up the companionway with Wes to find an angry ocean and a strong wind. With a few shouted consultations, they worked together to prepare for their trip back to the marina, quickly getting soaked by the rain. All the while her mind spun with the new perspective Wes had given her about her uncle and his actions.

Had Uncle Dan been ashamed that he'd literally been asleep on the job? Did he blame himself for what happened to her?

Maybe, she conceded. She'd thought he was angry because Roger had forced him to acknowledge that she wasn't the son or nephew he'd always wanted. She'd never forget the way he roared at her the last time she tried to board the *Amphitrite*. That banishment had cut her to the core. She'd thought her uncle was telling her she wasn't fit for the *Amphitrite*. That somehow she was tainted by her gender and by the way Roger treated her. Now she read it a different way.

Wes was right; Dan had thought his worth lay in his

strength and capabilities. His accident had worn away at his self-respect. He'd begun to bark at her if she tried to help him carry supplies or move heavy items on the boat. His drinking had undercut his health and his abilities even more.

When he'd realized Roger attacked her—and that he hadn't been awake to stop it—had he felt he'd failed her? Had he thought he'd failed at being a man?

Probably, Penelope conceded.

Maybe Wes had Dan pegged. Maybe he felt so bad about his own shortcomings he thought the only way to keep her safe was to banish her from the *Amphitrite* altogether.

If so, it changed everything, Penelope decided as she gripped the wheel and kept them on a steady course through the choppy water. The incident had scared her. It had given her bad dreams and made her more wary of men, but it hadn't overwhelmed her, and it certainly hadn't dimmed her desire to make her living on the *Amphitrite*. Now she wondered if she'd recovered so quickly because she had been able to knock Roger out. She'd come out of the incident shaken but with proof that her instincts were good.

Like Wes said, she'd identified Roger as a trouble-maker from the first moment they met. If it had been up to her, she would have sent him packing after his comment about her appearance. Even if she'd somehow missed the signs, she'd defended herself when he came after her. She wasn't dumb. She knew the outcome could have been different. Knew she couldn't protect herself if several men came at her at once.

That didn't mean she needed to stay ashore, however. It meant she needed to take the steps necessary to keep herself and everyone else aboard safe. That probably meant hiring someone to help with larger groups. Wes thought that was a reasonable solution.

Hell, Uncle Dan had never worked alone, either. He had her, and when she was at school or absent for other reasons, he brought someone else along. She could do that, too. Why had she ever felt that doing so would be admitting defeat? Was it because of the way her uncle had treated her?

It was, Penelope decided. His reaction to the events that day had her second-guessing all her choices. Now she was clear about her capabilities again. Her instincts were good. She was a competent fishing guide. She could learn to take charge even if she hired a cousin or two to help her.

"Thank you," she yelled over the noise of the engine and the howling of the wind.

"For what?" Wes asked.

"For everything." She couldn't explain it under these conditions, but she'd be sure to tell him exactly what she meant later when they were alone.

THE GOING WAS slow, and the return journey took twice

as long as the way out. By the time the marina came into view, Wes was relieved. Once or twice he'd considered what they'd do if the motor gave out or the wind grew even higher. The *Amphitrite* was a good vessel, but every boat had its limits.

Wes leaped onto the dock as soon as they pulled in and tied up the boat, not an easy task in this gale, then came back aboard to help Penelope set everything to rights. The marina was in chaos as they negotiated the maze of boat slips and headed for her car. Several boats had drifted from their moorings during the storm, and men were arguing about the damage caused in one incident. Possessions that hadn't been stowed away properly lay askew on the decks of several vessels they passed. A tarp had blown into the water, and a woman was trying to fish it out. Wes took a moment to help her, then hurried to join Penelope by the CRV.

"How about letting me drive? You've already done your fair share today."

She handed him the keys. He opened the passenger side door for her, fished around in the back and passed her a towel.

The drive home took forever as the last of the storm blew over. Several times Wes had to skirt fallen tree limbs, and he had to detour a few blocks out of the way to avoid an accident. Police had set up cones and were working with a tow truck to move a car with its windshield smashed in.

"Someone's having a bad day," Wes remarked.

"*We're* having a bad day. We're late."

"It's going to be okay," he said. It had to be.

Penelope didn't answer. Wes picked up speed. He needed to get her home.

The first indication that something was wrong at EdgeCliff Manor came when they parked the car, hurried to the door and found it locked, something that hadn't happened the entire time Olivia and her entourage had been in possession of the house.

Penelope indicated the proper key and stood shivering as he fumbled with the lock. "We didn't get the marshmallow roasting sticks," she said suddenly.

Hell, he'd forgotten all about those. "We'll say they were sold out. Jenny Kensington bought them all last week," he improvised, naming an up-and-coming film star. "That's why we're late. We drove even farther to check out another possible source for them."

"You think Amber will believe that?"

"We could always tell her the truth."

She shook her head. "She hates the idea of anyone else having fun."

When he pushed the door open, the house had an empty feel. "Is anyone here?" Penelope called tentatively. Wes put a finger to his lips.

"If they don't see us, we can sneak upstairs and get changed. Then when we come back down, we can pretend we've been here for ages," he whispered.

They made their way carefully down the hall to the staircase. Penelope placed a hand on the banister, then froze. "The great room," she whispered. "The sliding doors are open."

Wes peered around her and saw she was right. A cool, wet breeze blew in through the wide-open doors, making the great room and the deck one seamless space.

"What the hell?" he breathed. It was clear no one was around, so he changed course and headed that way.

"Oh, my God," Penelope said as she followed him.

The open doors had let the torrential rain blow straight inside. A quarter-inch of water covered most of the floor. The tower of speakers was soaking wet. So were the curtains. A mound of sheer cloth and ribbon meant to decorate the venue tomorrow was a heaping mass. The ink on a stack of hand-calligraphied name cards and menus had run, forming a dark spot on the hardwood floor.

A piles of boxes Amber had yet to open sagged in soggy towers. The pink paint so recently applied to the walls was streaked with rain.

"Why were the doors open?" Penelope asked. "Where is everyone? Olivia? Amber!" She stalked to the stairs and ran up to the second floor. "Hey, is anyone here?"

Wes held his breath. Had Olivia and her people taken off?

"Their stuff is still here." Penelope appeared on the

stairs again. "Did they just forget the back of the house was open?"

"Maybe it isn't as bad as it looks," Wes said, coming to meet her. "Let's get changed out of our wet clothes, then I'll mop everything up, and you can see what we might be able to salvage."

"We can't salvage this." Penelope didn't move, but her voice slid upward. "There's no way to salvage this— the wedding is tomorrow!"

"We can deal with the worst of it before Olivia and her people get home."

But even as he said the words, Penelope's phone buzzed. She pulled it out. "It's Amber."

Wes's heart sank. "Buy us some time."

SHE DESPERATELY NEEDED to change into dry clothes, Penelope thought as Amber's voice got ever shriller. The soaking-wet fabric stuck clammily to her skin, and every time she moved, its jellyfish grip clamped to a new part of her anatomy. Amber kept going on and on about how Penelope hadn't warned her about the storm.

"Tomorrow will be perfect. I swear," Penelope said loudly into the phone when it was clear Amber would never stop yelling.

"How can you know that?" Amber demanded. "You didn't know it would rain today! If tomorrow isn't perfect, Olivia and Vincent will probably fire me. And then I'll sue your ass."

"Where are you all, anyway?"

"Reminding the world that Olivia is still in Seahaven and that she's got a wedding coming up," Amber said as if Penelope should have known. "She had to be seen, which should have been easy, but this is a stupid little town, and no one even noticed Olivia and Vincent when they went shopping in the tourist district. The stores were practically empty, and then it started to pour. We're at a coffee shop now. Cups and Sailboats, or something like that."

"Cups & Waves? What about your workmen? There's no one here."

There was a brief pause. "Jerome says they're on their way."

"Here's what we'll do, then." Penelope thought fast. Wes was right; there was no way she could allow Amber to see the place like this. "I'm sending someone over to take you to the coolest places in town—the places people will see you and recognize Olivia and Vincent. Okay? You just sit tight."

"We're supposed to be back at the house now. My time line—"

"Publicity trumps time line," Penelope snapped. "Come on, Amber, wake up. You know that."

There was a shocked silence on the other end of the line.

"Someone will meet you at Cups & Waves in ten minutes," Penelope said again and hung up.

Wes had rounded up most of the towels in the house and started mopping up water.

"Go change," he told her.

"I'll change in a minute." First she called Emma and filled her in on the situation. Emma immediately offered to help and volunteered Noah to be tour guide. She brought him on the line. "I'll start by taking them to the pier. We can eat lunch at Surf Point," he said, naming one of Seahaven's fanciest restaurants. "Everyone is happier with a full stomach."

"Thank you," Penelope said.

"I'll be over in a minute to help," Emma said. "I'll bring food."

"You're a lifesaver."

"Go change," Wes said again when she ended her call.

"Fine. You'd better come, too." Who knew when they'd get a chance again? They hurried to the top floor, changed into dry things and threw their wet things onto the balcony. Penelope paced her apartment as Wes insisted on making them mugs of hot chocolate.

It occurred to her she had an opportunity here to wrest back a little control. While Wes finished in the kitchen, she returned to her bedroom and fetched the binder of swatches and paint colors she'd put together while renovating the house.

She rushed downstairs to the door when the workmen arrived. "We've got a lot to do and very little time to do it," she announced as she herded the men and women into the great room. "First things first. We need to repaint the walls. You five start prepping them. Wes, can you go to the hardware store?"

"On it." Wes downed his hot chocolate and headed out the door, paint swatches in hand.

She assigned more workers to move the sodden boxes onto the deck now that the rain had stopped and gave one man the job to lift the stain from the hardwood floor. Everyone else went to work mopping up the rest of the water.

The crew ran powerful fans to help dry the wood and carted off the sound system they couldn't have used anyway, which was a big relief, because Penelope was fairly certain Amber had meant to plug it in as soon as the reception started, no matter what she'd promised.

Wes soon returned with the paint. As soon as the crew started spreading it on the walls and ceiling, Penelope found she could breathe easier. That awful pink had been getting to her.

"Got it all out!" the man cleaning the ink stain from the floor said.

"Thank goodness." She gave him a hug before sending him to join the painting crew.

Emma took a load of towels to her place to wash. Penelope ran a load, too, but she doubted many of them could be saved. Emma had promised to run to the store and buy new sets for the guests.

"Penelope?" Wes said some time later. "What's in all these boxes?"

She came outside on the deck to see. Wes opened one and pulled out something that might have once been a garish pink paper flower but was now little more than a sodden mess.

"I'm pretty sure all those gauzy things were supposed to take the place of flowers, decorations and table linens."

"Table linens, huh?"

Penelope sagged against the wall, staggered by this new set of problems. She wasn't prepared with any decor of her own that would appeal to Olivia. For a minute her fears threatened to overcome her. She could just see the reviews EdgeCliff Manor would get.

"Would Emma or Ava have some?" Wes asked.

"They might." Penelope thought about it, then straightened. "I know who to call." She dialed Kate's number. "I've got an emergency," she said and explained everything. "I need flowers, table linens, decorations. Do you have any ideas?" Kate had been one of Emma's first guests. She'd fallen in love with Seahaven and decided to stay and open a landscaping business. Now she had contacts all over town.

"I'll figure it out," Kate said. "I can call around to the nurseries. I'll call you back to sort out details after I do a little research."

"Thanks. Olivia likes pink," she added.

"Of course. Everyone knows that," Kate said.

When she cut the call, Penelope noticed Wes's frown. "What?" she demanded.

"Tablecloths mean tables, right? Where are they?"

Penelope's heart sank. Amber was supposed to supply those. She texted Noah. *Can you find out where Amber is securing tables from? Pretend you need some for an upcoming event.*

From a company called Celebrations in San Jose, he texted back a few minutes later. Penelope tried them, but their line was busy the first few times. Finally she got through.

"Yes?" a harried voice answered.

"My table delivery didn't arrive." Penelope wondered what else hadn't shown up.

"No one's deliveries arrived," the woman said. "There's a mudslide covering the highway. Who knows when it will be cleaned up."

Penelope absorbed this new blow. "What about Highway 1?" They'd have to circle hours out of their way to reach it, but then they could travel down the coast to Seahaven."

"There's a pileup on Highway 1. Half our crew didn't even make it to work. We're doing our best, but I can't guarantee we'll get there today. Can you hold?" The line switched to playing scratchy classical music. Penelope hung up.

"No tables. No nothing if it's a delivery coming in from San Jose," she announced. She quickly tapped the screen of her phone and brought up a local social media site. Sure enough, a mudslide covered the road, and the accident on Highway 1 looked like it wouldn't be cleared any time soon. Having lived in the area all her life, she was used to these periodic disasters, but they'd never happened at such an inopportune time before.

"What do we do?" Wes asked.

Penelope thought a moment. "I don't know." She texted Noah, who confirmed Olivia and her entourage were being served their meals right then.

Where can I get tables?

She waited for Noah's reply.

We've got a couple of folding ones, Noah texted back. *I bet lots of people do. Call Colette Rainer.*

It was a smart suggestion. Colette ran Heaven on Earth farm and had lived in Seahaven all her life. When she heard what was happening, she told Penelope not to worry. "I'll get you plenty of tables. I've got linens and place settings, too, if you need them."

"Thank you. Do you know Kate Lindsay? Can you coordinate with her?"

"Of course."

Penelope gave Colette all the details, then hung up. She knew she should feel relieved, but the truth was she was getting more and more nervous. The eclectic, homespun wedding she was putting together would have been perfect for any of her friends, but it bore no resemblance to the extravaganza Olivia wanted. What if she flat-out refused to accept the substitutions?

Sooner than she expected, friends of Colette began stopping by with tables, linens and place settings. Colette was one of the last to arrive with a truck full of everything they might need. Kate arrived with a van full of flowers that had been donated by local businesses. Emma stopped by with bags of new towels and platters of sandwiches for the hungry workers.

"My guests aren't going to make it this weekend," she told Penelope. "They heard about the mudslide and decided to postpone their trip since it will be hard to get here from the airport. That frees me up to help tomorrow night, too."

"Thank you," Penelope said.

"See? I told you it would all work out," Wes said when it was three thirty in the afternoon and they were finally making headway.

"So far, so good." The real test would come when Olivia arrived.

Her phone chimed. *I'll have Olivia and Vincent home within the hour,* Noah texted.

The phone chimed again. *Finally!* Amber texted. *Some photos of Olivia and Vincent are getting lots of attention!*

Penelope wasn't sure what to think about that. She clicked the link Amber sent her.

"Oh, my goodness. Look." She held up the phone so Emma and Wes could see. The photo showed Olivia and Vincent enthusiastically, though not exactly skillfully, attempting to surf. Amber sent another link, this one to a short movie of them catching another wave, both of them pitching into the water at the end of the clip.

You took Olivia and Vincent surfing? she texted to Noah.

Hanging out in cafes and restaurants just wasn't piquing anyone's interest. I got some of the Surf Moms and Dads to give them a lesson. Told all of them to post the photos I took on social media. They started to trend. There's a big crowd here now.

That's great, Penelope texted back, but she wasn't sure it was. On the one hand, if she didn't get media attention, Olivia would be devastated. On the other hand, she might not want the humble little wedding they were about to throw her to be beamed to a huge audience.

Penelope looked around again. The room was bright and cheerful with its new coat of paint. The ceiling was back to a flat white. The floorboards were drying. The deck was full of tables, and decorations were piling up, ready for tomorrow. Emma and Kate were crafting arrangements from a variety of candles and flowers.

It was a miracle they'd managed as much as they'd had, but she doubted Olivia would see it that way.

"What's wrong?" Wes came to fold her in his arms and murmured the question in her ear.

"This isn't going to work," she said, keeping her voice low. She leaned back against him, savoring his strength. "It just isn't. Olivia is brash and bold. Modern. Ahead of the game, even. We're making her a small-town, old-fashioned homemade wedding. As lovely as it's going to be, it will be all wrong for her."

After a moment he nodded. "I don't want to admit it, but I see what you mean."

"I have to think of something to salvage this, but I'm out of ideas."

"Okay, let's brainstorm. We still have time."

Penelope's phone dinged. Another text from Noah. *Moving more quickly than I thought. We'll be home in ten.*

"WHO WAS THAT?" Wes asked when Penelope's phone chimed and she frowned.

"It's Noah again. We've got ten minutes. That's not enough time."

"Take a breath. It's going to be okay." He braced himself, waiting for her to contradict him. He knew what she meant when she said Olivia wasn't going to like what they'd done. He had no doubt Penelope and her friends would manage to pull off a gorgeous event, but that wasn't what Olivia wanted. She was aiming for a wedding that would stand out on social media.

A loud knock prevented Penelope from answering him. "Now what?"

"I'll get that." He hurried down the hall, figuring it was a delivery person, since he knew neither Amber nor Olivia would have bothered to knock, even if they managed to get back so soon. When he opened the door, however, he found his parents standing outside.

This was bad. "What are you two doing here?" He looked from one to the other. "Is Grace okay?"

"She's fine." His mom didn't sound too happy, though. "I don't see why you're worried about her; we're the ones who are up a creek without a paddle."

Belatedly, Wes realized they expected him to invite them in, but he didn't see how he could. Penelope was stressed enough without uninvited guests showing up.

"Look, we're having a bit of a crisis here, so I'll need to send you back to your hotel. We can connect later."

"That's not going to work for us," his father said. "We need you back in New Jersey. Now."

Irritation buzzed through his veins. Why couldn't his parents ever listen to him? "I don't have time for this right now," he reiterated. Instead of letting them in, he stepped outside and shut the door behind him, cursing himself for listing the address of Fisherman's Point in the email he'd sent his father a year ago.

"You have to have time," his dad said. "We're under a deadline, and we need you to act like a team player. You think you can survive if you go out on your own like some free agent? That's not how the world works, bud. Family is everything, something your sister forgot. I expect better from you."

The same lecture he'd been getting since he was a child and didn't get the grades they expected him to get. He'd let down the family by not doing well enough in school, not getting an MBA, not proving to be useful to the company. He'd been so close to breaking free before Grace decided to steal that money.

"I made a commitment to a friend, and I'm carrying it out." Time was passing. Penelope needed him. Olivia would be back any minute.

"What about the commitment you made to us?" his mother asked. "For once in your life, would you put us first? Is that too much to ask?"

"We've bent over backward to accommodate your penchant for running off who knows where," his father said. "What other company in the world would pay you the salary we do while you're slacking off all the time? It's downright embarrassing."

It was. Wes had a hard time looking his coworkers in the face when he showed up at Abbott Enterprises. He knew how ridiculous it was that he was paid for doing practically nothing, and he couldn't tell anyone he was being paid not to get a job somewhere else. Who would understand that?

Damn his parents and their pride. Why had he ever gone along with it? He was sick of feeling ashamed of himself. Sick of having to hide what he really wanted.

Sick of his debt to them hanging over his head.

"I can't do this tonight," he said. "Go back to your hotel. I'll call you on Sunday when I'm free." He could deal with them after the wedding.

"On Sunday?" His mother lifted her hands in disbelief.

"That's right." He stared her down.

"But—" His father broke off when a limo pulled up

and parked in the road, halfway blocking Wes's parents' rental car. Olivia, Amber, Vincent, Noah and several other people climbed out.

"Did the party start without us?" Olivia called. She sounded a little bleary, like maybe the surfing had taken it out of her.

"Everyone knows there's no party without you," Wes called back, affecting a hearty tone he didn't feel. "These are my parents. They were just leaving."

"Ooh, Wes has parents!" Olivia cooed.

"Most people do," his mother said tartly.

"I don't," Olivia said and kept going into the house. Vincent saluted them and followed her, looking a little worse for wear, too.

Amber brought up the rear, Noah on her heels. "I hope everything is under control here," she said caustically.

Inside, Olivia screamed.

CHAPTER 11

"*E*VERYBODY NEEDS TO calm down," Penelope said for the third time. "Like I said, there was nothing we could do but clean up the mess. It's no one's fault there was a surprise rainstorm. If you had closed the doors before you left—"

"You're blaming us?" Amber rounded on her. "It's not our fault, it's yours. You're in charge of everything that happens here. It's your responsibility to keep us satisfied."

"And I'm not satisfied," Olivia shrieked.

"We've done the best we could with short notice and no resources. I think we've done a very good job. The venue is classically beautiful. The decor is soft and sweet—"

"Olivia Raquette isn't soft or sweet," Amber said. "Olivia Raquette is flashy, new, bright, on trend."

"She's not *on-trend*. She's a *trend-setter*," Penelope said desperately. "She'll start a new trend. Romantic getaway weddings."

"That's not a new trend! That's the oldest trick in the

book!" Amber threw up her hands. "That's it! The wedding is off!"

Penelope felt like she'd been punched. Olivia looked like she'd been. For one split second, her control vanished, replaced by—panic. Penelope followed her gaze to Vincent. The brash young celebrity looked equally startled, for a moment appearing even younger than he usually did, before he schooled his expression into his usual proud pout.

Olivia's and Vincent's dismay stopped Penelope in her tracks. With all the insanity this week, she'd forgotten that these two young people planned to pledge their love to each other tomorrow. Olivia and Vincent might be little more than children, and she'd wondered more than once if this was all a meaningless publicity stunt, but now she thought maybe she had it wrong.

"Vincent, do you love Olivia?" she asked.

"Y-yeah."

"Olivia, do you love Vincent?"

"Of course."

"Then *you* don't get to call off their wedding," Penelope told Amber. "It's up to Olivia and Vincent what to do next." She turned back to them. "Olivia, you've got a choice to make. What's more important, Vincent or the color of the walls?"

"Yeah, babe," Vincent chimed in. "What's more important?"

Olivia pursed her lips. "You," she admitted.

"Vincent, what's more important, Olivia or that video game upstairs?"

He drew back. "That video game is my career."

Penelope waited.

"Olivia," he said grudgingly. "I don't know why I have to choose, though."

"Because we've got a ton left to do before the wedding tomorrow, and I need both of you to pitch in. That means no more gaming until after the reception. Understand?"

He heaved a sigh. "Fine."

"Here's the thing," Penelope said. "Tomorrow when you say your vows, you aren't going to be thinking about photographers or influencers, Olivia. You're going to be thinking about the life you're about to build with Vincent."

"I guess."

"And, Vincent, you sure as heck aren't going to be thinking about video games when Olivia is saying her vows to you."

He glanced at his bride. Something softened in him. "Yeah."

"Olivia, do you think a homespun wedding could be your thing?" Penelope went on.

"I don't know. I wanted something really… special."

Her wistfulness caught Penelope in the heart, and she knew all her persuasion couldn't change the truth. She could probably keep pushing and maybe persuade

Olivia to go ahead with the wedding the way it stood, but Olivia was right.

This wasn't special.

"This is all very sweet," Amber said, her tone indicating it wasn't. "But aren't you forgetting one very important thing?"

"What's that?"

"The guests? If the highway is closed, how will they get here from the airport?" Amber crossed her arms and raised her eyebrows.

Penelope closed her eyes. The guests. Amber was right; she'd completely forgotten them.

"Really?" Amber pushed on. "You don't have some magical homespun answer for that problem, too?"

Olivia waited hopefully, as if she thought Penelope just might.

"No," Penelope admitted in a whisper. "I don't."

"Sure you do," Wes spoke up. He turned to Amber. "You know Penelope has a boat, right?"

The *Amphitrite*. Penelope's mouth dropped open. She'd forgotten all about her—and the *Amphitrite* could solve two problems at once. "We'll have the wedding on the boat," she cried. "It'll be perfect. You won't believe what we can do with it, Olivia. There will be lights strung up. We'll head out on the ocean. You'll say your vows at sea." Just like her cousin Jason's wedding she'd loved so much.

"That sounds cool." Vincent perked up.

"It… does," Olivia said.

"That's a fabulous idea." Emma spoke for the first time.

"I think so, too," Noah said.

"Your guests can take a different highway from the airport to Monterey. We'll travel down the coast, fetch them from there and hold the ceremony as we return," Wes said. "We can time it to happen as the sun goes down, then wind the party up back here."

"What do you think?" Penelope asked Olivia and held her breath.

Olivia smiled—a real smile for once. "I think that sounds perfect."

"Then let's get to work."

CHAPTER 12

"*Y*OU MAY NOW kiss the bride," Kamirah said. She looked like a cross between a queen and a fairy godmother today, Wes thought, with her braids in a coronet on top of her head, pink ribbons woven among them. Olivia's original officiant, the head of an organization in Humboldt County Wes suspected was a cult, had cancelled when he heard about the mudslide. Colette was the one who suggested they call Kamirah. "That young woman isn't just a barista. She has her fingers in a lot of pies," she'd told them. "If you ever need a doula, she can do that, too."

Vincent wrapped Olivia in an embrace and kissed her with feeling. Wes squeezed Penelope's hand. He'd taken it early in the ceremony and hadn't let go, needing to keep her close. His time at EdgeCliff Manor was nearly over, and he didn't want to leave.

Couldn't stand the thought of leaving.

He'd managed to get rid of his parents yesterday when Olivia screamed, reiterating that his help was needed inside. He was glad he'd been able to suggest using the *Amphitrite* to solve the problems Penelope was facing. The more Olivia and Vincent pitched in to help prepare for the wedding, the happier the young couple became. They'd gone down to the marina, and Penelope had assigned Olivia and Vincent the task of stringing the lights around the *Amphitrite*. They'd done so enthusiastically, laughing and teasing each other as they went.

"See?" Olivia had said when they were done. "I'm capable of far more than being looked at."

"You're right," Vincent had said. "You're the best. I don't know why I ever said that."

"I want you to be proud of me."

"I want you to be proud of me, too."

Wes had slipped away then, leaving them to their private discussion. For the first time, he'd thought maybe their relationship stood a chance.

Now he shifted his gaze from the happy couple to the woman who had grown so dear to him in so short a time. He'd held Penelope in his arms the last three nights, but it wasn't nearly enough. He couldn't imagine a life without her.

He hated to think of disappointing his parents, but the pain that sliced through his heart at the thought of leaving Penelope behind told him everything he needed to know. He'd do what he could to smooth things over with his folks, but he wasn't going to walk away from this chance at happiness.

His fingers tightened around Penelope's again as

conviction filled him. Now that he'd made a decision, he couldn't see how he could have made any other choice. He had no idea what Penelope would think. Maybe she wouldn't want him as a partner. Maybe this wouldn't work out—

It had to, Wes decided. He couldn't stand the alternative.

He loved Penelope, just as he'd told her on the *Amphitrite*. She hadn't said the words back to him. Maybe she never would.

It didn't matter.

She was the woman he'd give anything to protect. The one he wanted to spend his life making happy. He wanted to share his days with her—his nights, too. Maybe they could start a family.

Maybe he'd finally know what it was to have a home.

When the happy couple broke apart, Vincent tipped his head back and howled. "Yeah! She's mine now, suckers!"

Olivia playfully elbowed her new husband, but she was smiling. Wes thought she looked truly happy. Several drones hovered overhead capturing footage of the event as the speakers Amber had installed around the *Amphitrite* began to blast music. They'd picked up the most important guests from Monterey. Several more fishing vessels had picked up the rest of them. At the moment they were stationed nearby, their passengers applauding as Vincent and Olivia kissed again. Together, the little fleet would travel back up the coast to Seahaven, where Kate, Aurora and some of the Surf Moms were putting the last touches on EdgeCliff Manor while they were away. Emma and Ava were catering the affair with the help of the ladies from Heaven on Earth farm. They would be busy at Emma's place, getting the meal in order.

Wes's parents were texting him every half hour, but he wasn't answering them. Time enough to tell them his news tomorrow. He squeezed Penelope's hand again. Everything he wanted was right here, and that's what he was focusing on today.

Back at EdgeCliff Manor, he alternated between being useful and enjoying the reception. As soon as Emma's food was served and the drinks got flowing, a cheerful hum of chatter and laughter announced the success of the gathering. Kate and Aurora had brought so many more flowers today, they ended up handing out the extras to the guests. Soon flower crowns and boutonnieres were the order of the day. Amber had somehow found a replacement sound system. The backyard was decked with fairy lights, lending a magical air to the proceedings.

"It looks like something out of a storybook," he heard a guest say, and pride for Penelope swelled his chest. She'd pulled this off—with help—when it could have been a disaster.

After dinner the tables were moved to the lawn and

the deck was set up for dancing. Olivia and Vincent took their place at the heart of it and began a classic waltz accompanied by a string quartet, but just when Wes was settling in to enjoy it, the sound system kicked in and the music changed pace. The bride ripped the long panels of her skirts away, revealing a much more up-to-date minidress, and she and Vincent began a choreographed, fast-paced, whirlwind dance of shaking hips, lifts, twirls and more.

"How do they know how to do that?" Wes asked Penelope, who'd come to stand beside him.

"I don't know. I guess that's why they're the celebrities. Oh, those are the dance moves that made Olivia famous," she added as the music shifted again and one of Olivia's hits began to play.

The crowd cheered.

When the music slowed down and other guests flooded the deck, he asked if Penelope would join him. She looked around, making sure there were no fires to put out, and nodded her assent.

She felt good in his arms, as always, and soon he was wishing they were alone.

"How late do you think this thing will go?"

"I've told Amber that Vincent and Olivia should head out by midnight, so we can disperse the guests by one. I don't think we can push it later than that without someone making a fuss."

"Sounds good." By one in the morning, he'd have

her alone, he vowed to himself.

And he meant to make the most of it.

They'd had a hell of a couple of days, but his desire to be with Penelope hadn't dimmed a bit. He wanted to be alone with her. Wanted to tell her how he felt.

He was never going back to New Jersey. Would never be CEO of Abbott Enterprises.

If Penelope would have him, he was going to stay right here.

"YOU PULLED IT off," Emma said when Penelope met up with her and Ava later that evening by the dessert platters they'd set out on folding tables in the great room. Her friends kept slipping off to Emma's house and coming back with more as fast as the guests could eat them.

"*We* pulled it off," Penelope corrected her. "I never could have done this without all your help."

"You got a baptism by fire, didn't you?" Emma laughed. "At least you know your next wedding won't be so dramatic."

"There won't be another wedding," Penelope said. "I'm going to be a fishing guide." The last twenty-four hours had cemented the idea in her mind. Wes was right; it wasn't her fault Roger Atlas attacked her. There was no reason to give up her dreams because Uncle Dan had felt guilty for not preventing the incident. This was her life. The *Amphitrite* was her boat now. She was in charge, and she knew which way her path lay.

"You are?" Ava clapped her hands. "Penelope, that's wonderful!"

"You really think so?"

"I know so. You've never seemed happy when you talked about holding weddings at EdgeCliff Manor, but every time you talk about the *Amphitrite* or fishing, you glow."

"If you were sitting on the Trouble Bench, do you know what I would say?" Emma asked.

"What?"

"What took you so long?"

"Seriously? That's all the advice I'd get? Where's my glass of water, at least?"

Emma laughed and fetched her a bottle from a cooler.

"You're right," Penelope said after she took a long drink. "I guess I made a mountain out of a molehill when I thought Uncle Dan could dictate what I did after he was gone."

"You cared about his opinion. He was like a father to you," Emma said. "It's not strange at all that you'd have reservations given everything that happened, but in the end you have to listen to your own gut."

"And your gut loves fishing," Ava said.

"The rest of me does, too," Penelope said.

"Does that mean you're going to renovate all over again?" Ava asked.

"Yeah, are you bringing back that old linoleum?" Emma teased.

"No linoleum. But I do want my kitchen back."

"Of course you do. It's a beautiful kitchen. I like that you've put your own spin on Fisherman's Point. I bet you'll get a lot more couples and families coming to fish than your uncle did, now that this place is spiffed up," Emma said. "The women will feel comfortable here. It's so clean and bright and welcoming."

"Thank you. I think you're right."

"Uh-oh. Incoming," Ava said.

Penelope braced herself for Amber's next demand when she saw who was coming, but instead the woman held up her phone. "Departure in ten minutes. The limo is already out front." She nodded to a couple of men coming down the stairs carrying luggage. "That's the last of our things."

"We'll wind the party down as soon as you're gone," Penelope said. "If we find anything that belongs to you, I'll box it up and send it."

"You have my number. My workmen will be here in the morning to get your home back to rights." Amber turned as if to go, then stopped and looked back over her shoulder. "You did good." With a curt nod, she strode out into the throng dancing on the deck, leaving Penelope a little stunned. She *had* done good, she decided. The wedding was a success. Photos of the event were already trending on social media. Olivia and

Vincent were over the moon.

She could handle whatever the future held.

THE LAST OF the guests were trailing drunkenly out the door, ushered into waiting cabs by Noah and Sam, when Wes's parents arrived. They picked their way past the partiers and entered the house before Wes could stop them, herding him into the great room, where a number of Penelope's friends were helping to clean up now that the crowds of guests were gone. Penelope, Ava and Emma had just left carrying platters of leftover food to Emma's house.

"What are you doing here?" he demanded.

"Coming to talk to you," his father said testily. "We've been trying to reach you all day."

"I told you I'd get in touch tomorrow. I've been busy." He indicated the aftermath of the reception. Kate, Aurora and Connor were walking around with trays collecting beer bottles and glassware. Edie, Marta and the rest of the Surf Moms were folding chairs and sweeping up. The Surf Dads were breaking down the tables. He hadn't had a chance yet to talk to Penelope, either. Not that it mattered. Even if she didn't want him to stay, that wouldn't change anything regarding his future with Abbott Enterprises.

"This can't wait. I can't understand whether you're being deliberately obtuse or you're just stupid. We're in a crisis, Wes. We need your help."

"You have to listen to us," his mother added. "It turns out your sister is sneakier than we thought and—"

"Wes?" Noah shouted from the door. "The police just showed up!"

Now? Had someone called during the last minutes of the party to complain?

"I need to handle this," he told his parents.

His parents exchanged a look. "Of course. Forget we were even here," his mother said hurriedly. She took his father's arm and guided him quickly out the back to the deck. "We'll get out of your hair," she added in such a falsely cheerful voice, Wes stared back at her. His mother was never cheerful.

"You're going the wrong way—hey!" Wes protested as two armed men swiftly pushed past him and caught up with his parents. "What's going on?"

"IRS-CI Special Agent-in-Charge," one of the men snapped, flashing a badge at him without missing a beat. He grabbed Wes's father's arm and folded it behind his back.

"What?" Wes couldn't keep up. Why was the IRS sending special agents to here? And why were they going after his folks?

"This is all a mistake. You've got the wrong people," his father said to the uniformed man who snapped cuffs around his wrists and corralled him into the house.

"Don't touch me! I'm not a criminal," his mother shrieked at the agent arresting her.

Wes didn't know what do. He wanted to step in and stop what was happening, but he had a feeling it would make everything worse. He tuned in to what the special agent-in-charge was saying. "—failure to obey summons. You'll have to come with us."

"What summons?" Wes asked. "Mom? Dad? What summons?" He wasn't sure what the IRS-CI was, but it had to have something to do with paying taxes.

"This is all your sister's fault. And yours," his dad huffed as the agents hustled him past Wes. Wes trailed them through the house and stood by helplessly as his mother and father were loaded into a waiting vehicle.

"What am I supposed to do now?" he asked one of the agents as they rounded the van.

"Call a lawyer if you've got one."

Then they were gone.

Wes watched the official vehicles' taillights disappear down the road. He pulled out his phone. His parents had a lawyer, but it was past three in the morning back east. Should he call him now or wait a few hours?

"Wes?" a familiar voice called softly.

Wes spun around. "Who's there?"

When his sister stepped out from behind another parked car, he couldn't even manage to be surprised.

"I don't understand what's happening," he said.

She moved closer until he could make out her face. "Like I told you. I didn't embezzle any money. I discovered Mom and Dad were committing tax fraud—

for years. That's what I've been trying to tell you. Last February, a junior accountant pigeon-holed me at a party. He mentioned a few discrepancies he'd seen. As soon as I checked into one or two things he said, I found out he was right. I kept it quiet at first. I wanted to catch the culprit and bring the evidence to Mom and Dad. And then I realized it was them."

Wes shook his head. Why would his parents do that?

"They had two sets of books, Wes," she said when she saw he didn't believe her. "I found the proof on one of their home computers. When I confronted them, they told me everyone did it. They expected me to help them cover it up. Turned out I wasn't the only one who figured it out, though. The IRS did, too. Mom and Dad wanted to sacrifice me to shield them."

"They said that?"

She nodded. "When I refused, they fired me."

He heard a world of pain in her voice, and Wes could only imagine how she'd felt. She'd spent a lifetime being the daughter they wanted her to be, thinking that was the way to their hearts. At the first sign of trouble, they'd thrown her to the wolves.

Now you owe me.

Wes heard his father's voice in his mind, and a dismaying truth struck him. Even when he was twenty-two, his parents were making sure they had a way to keep him in the fold. He was the ace up their sleeves, so to speak.

"They always knew they could count on me if you

ever failed them," he said slowly. "That's why they kept me as VP even though I didn't deserve it. That's why they've been trying to get me home. No one outside the company would think twice if they promoted me when you left, since I worked there for a decade, but they weren't bringing me in now as CEO because I'd be great at the job. They wanted me because they knew I'd be lousy at it. I'd never notice discrepancies in their bookkeeping. I'd say whatever they told me to say. I'd be the clueless frontman for the company, while they lurked in the background doing whatever the hell they wanted." If he had noticed something, his father would have brought up the *Loose Cannon*. He would have called in that debt, thinking he could shame Wes into going along with their lies if nothing else worked.

Grace shook her head. "They were underestimating you. You would have figured it out sooner or later."

Would he? Wes wasn't sure. Telecommunications held no interest for him. Neither did accounting of any kind. It was the ocean that called to him. The air and sun and breeze and the science and art of fishing all entranced him in a way spreadsheets and projections and corporate decision-making never had.

He was good at the things he was passionate about, but he was lousy at the things he wasn't. That was simply who he was.

His parents had been prepared to capitalize on that.

"What's going to happen now?" he asked, ignoring

the pain that tightened his chest.

"There will be an investigation. We'll be audited. It would probably help if you and I presented a united front to show the company is in good hands now. Still, I think we're going to have to sell Abbott Enterprises."

Wes straightened. "Are you sure? You love that business."

"This is going to be in the headlines tomorrow. As long as an Abbott is in charge of the company, it will be tainted. We'll have to pay back taxes and interest, and the company is going to take a financial hit, but it's still worth a lot. I'll work on Mom and Dad. I'll get them to see the best path forward. When the company is sold, they'll have plenty of money. I don't know if they'll have to serve jail time, or simply pay some fines, but at the end of the day there should still be enough for them to retire on."

He couldn't imagine his frenetically busy parents calling it a day on work—or spending time in jail, for that matter—but he supposed that was their problem, not his. It stunned him to realize how little they'd cared about his safety or reputation—or Grace's. Would they really have let her go to jail in their place?

He couldn't fathom that.

"What about you?" he asked his sister.

"I guess it's time for me to strike out on my own."

Wes invited her inside. No sense standing on the stoop having this discussion. She followed him down the hall to the great room.

"That junior accountant I told you about?" she added. "His name is Bryan. We've been dating. We're talking about making it a permanent arrangement."

"Good for you." Wes wasn't sure how many more surprises he could take. He was exhausted. He realized as he looked around there wasn't anywhere to sit. He went to fetch a couple of the borrowed chairs from the lawn and set them up in a corner of the room where they'd be out of the way of the rest of the people cleaning up.

"Bryan has been talking about starting his own firm," Grace said. "Maybe I'll join him. Or maybe I'll do something else."

"I'm sorry for everything you had to go through," Wes said. "I should have listened to you when you called. I shouldn't have made you deal with this on your own." Grace was holding up well under the circumstances. He felt like a landmine had exploded beneath his feet.

"How about we start over?" she suggested. "I'll stop resenting you, and you stop keeping me at a distance."

"Sounds like a good plan." There were just the two of them now. He couldn't imagine ever feeling like his parents were part of his family again.

Penelope came back then, and Wes's anguish diminished a little. He introduced her to his sister and got her up to date on all that had happened while she was at Emma's house.

"I sit down with my friends for fifteen minutes and

the police show up?" Penelope shook her head.

"The IRS, actually," Wes told her. "Guess no one complained about the noise tonight."

"Thank goodness for small mercies."

By the time Grace left for her hotel and the rest of their helpers went home, Wes could hardly keep his eyes open. Penelope looked equally exhausted, but he couldn't go to bed until he'd told her everything. They took drinks to the third-floor balcony, changed into comfortable clothes and sat listening to the crash of waves on the beach far below them. Wes relayed to her everything Grace had told him and some of his own thoughts from earlier in the day.

"I'd already made a decision before my parents showed up," he finished, "and now I'm more set on it than ever."

"What decision?"

"I'm a fishing guide, not a CEO. That's what I'm meant to be, and it's what I want to do. I'm not going back to New Jersey, Penelope. I want to stay here. I'd like to work for you."

A smile spread over her face. "You want to stay?"

"That's right."

"And you want to work for me?"

"If you'll have me."

"That's a wonderful coincidence."

"What do you mean?"

"I decided today I'm a fishing guide, too. Not a boutique wedding venue owner."

"Oh, yeah? Don't suppose you have a boat."

"Actually, I do. And I could use some help." She touched his arm.

"So, you're hiring?"

"I am."

"Does the job come with accommodations?"

"It does." Her smile widened.

"There's this little third-floor bedroom I've come to like a lot. I don't suppose that's the place?"

"It is." She grinned at him. "It'll be like being on vacation every day."

"There might be unruly guests," he reminded her.

"They can't be worse than Olivia."

They both knew that wasn't true, but Wes let it slide. "Together I figure we can handle just about anything." He took Penelope's hand. "There's something else I need to tell you."

"What's that?"

"I love you, Penelope Rider. And some day I'm going to ask you to marry me."

"You know what? I love you, too."

CHAPTER 13

May

"*Y*OU'RE NOT GOING fishing today?" Emma asked. "How will you survive?"

"Ha ha," Penelope said. She was used to her friends' teasing. Ever since Olivia's well-documented wedding on the *Amphitrite*, she'd been inundated with requests for similar events—and her fishing charter business had taken off, too. Women preferred her as a guide. Men booked her services when they wanted to convince their wives or girlfriends that fishing wasn't that bad. She'd even had all-female parties who wanted a memorable—and photographable—girls' weekend on the boat.

She'd been amazed at how Amber's workmen had put the house in order after Olivia's wedding. Amber had even sent Penelope's painting to a restoration service, who'd returned it to her as good as new. Now she had both paintings hanging in the great room and frequently referred her guests to the artist's website when they exclaimed over them.

Wes's help made running the business easy—and

enjoyable. Just like they had from the beginning, they found they complemented each other well. They were both easygoing but didn't put up with trouble from customers. They were both conscientious and hardworking. They liked early mornings, loved being out in the elements and put their clients' safety above everything. They mostly booked fishing trips, but now and then they allowed a wedding into their schedule, too. They had enough experience it wasn't so daunting these days, but Penelope still preferred a fishing rod in her hands.

They'd become so popular, they had few openings in their schedule at all, but Wes had marked this day off on their calendar months ago. It was a bright May morning, and Penelope felt happy to be alive. She, Emma and Ava were on their way home from their usual morning walk. The men were surfing. The sun had slipped over the horizon a half hour ago as they started out, and the day stretched in front of her.

"Wes is taking me on a picnic," she told them. "We're going over to Castle Bluff. It should be lovely there today."

"Definitely," Ava said.

"I actually knew about the picnic," Emma confessed. "Wes asked me to pack a basket for you two. I made up the yummiest lunch I could."

"Emma's picnics are the best," Ava said.

"I can't wait."

A small sound came from the fabric sling Emma

wore strapped across her body. She stopped and checked on baby Sophia, who was born just two weeks earlier. Her birth went smoothly. Penelope thought it was amazing Emma was already back to taking their morning walks, but there was no stopping her.

Penelope bent to get a look at Sophia's tiny face. "I want a baby." She felt rather than saw her friends swap a look over her head. "I know—I'm putting the cart before the horse."

"Have you talked about having kids with Wes?"

"Only vaguely. We both want to be parents."

"I do, too," Ava said. "Which is a very good thing, because I'm going to be one."

Penelope straightened. "You are?"

Ava nodded.

"Congratulations!" Penelope pulled Ava into a hug. Emma did her best to throw her arms around both of them without squashing Sophia.

"When are you due?" Emma asked her.

"December. It'll be a holiday baby! I'm so excited."

"Of course you are!"

Their walk home was full of questions and explanations. Penelope was happy for her friend, but she was a little wistful, too, and by the time she left the others and returned to EdgeCliff Manor, she felt a restlessness she couldn't quite push aside. She threw in a load of wash, ran the vacuum cleaner around the first two floors and spent some time polishing the floor-to-ceiling sliding glass doors that led out to the deck, but the feeling hadn't passed by the time she met Wes at their agreed-on time. She found him hefting a heavy-looking basket into the trunk of his car.

"Emma packed us enough food for an army," he announced and came to take her hand. He leaned in for a kiss, and she tilted her face up to meet him. Everything always felt better when Wes was around. Maybe she'd broach the topic of their future today. Spending time together away from their work seemed like a good opportunity for a discussion like that.

Wes drove them across town to the high bluffs where Seahaven Castle stood. They parked in the large parking lot to the side of its tall walls and walked to the front end of the castle, where it faced the ocean.

A large, grassy open area between the castle walls and the edge of the bluffs was the site of a farmers market on Saturdays, but today the area was empty except for several other people taking advantage of the beautiful weather and views. Wes led the way to a spot far from the others, where Penelope spread the blanket she had brought along.

Together they unpacked the basket, exclaiming over the amount and variety of food Emma had prepared. By the time they'd worked through several appetizers and a main course of rustic sandwiches, chips and dip, crudites and hummus and much more, Penelope's good mood was restored.

"Remember the day we met?" Wes asked.

"Ugh. Yes." Penelope laughed. "As soon as you said you had a reservation, I just wanted to die. I knew it had to be true because Uncle Dan was such a lousy record-keeper, and Olivia and Amber were already being so unreasonable."

"Are you sorry you let me stay?"

"Of course not. It was the best decision I've ever made," she assured him.

"Really?"

"You know it's true."

"I'm glad you feel that way. I like living with you. Like working for you, too. I like everything about our life together."

Warmth blossomed within her chest. He was saying everything out loud she'd been thinking since they set out on this picnic.

But when Wes shifted onto one knee and took her hand, she was so surprised she gasped aloud.

"Penelope, would you make me the happiest man on earth? Would you marry me so we can keep doing everything we're doing for the rest of our lives?"

"Yes," Penelope said. She didn't have to think it over for a second. She wanted to be with Wes forever. Wanted this life to go on and on and on.

Wes drew her into his arms, and they kissed. Penelope didn't think she could contain her happiness, but when they drew apart, she said. "I've been thinking about babies." She thought it best to get that out in the open right away, in case Wes had other ideas.

She held her breath, but when Wes grinned, all her fears melted away.

"I can think about babies," he said and kissed her again. "I can think about them any old time. I can do more than think about them."

Penelope laughed. "That's good to know. Wes— we're in public."

"Too bad." He was circling her with his arms, tracing kisses down her neck, making it clear he was ready to get started making babies any time she wanted one. He sighed when he pulled back a minute later. "Okay, I'll behave. For now. Let's finish our picnic. Then we need to go find you a ring. I know just where to go."

"Where Emma and Ava got theirs?"

Wes nodded. "You know it. Two happy customers can't be wrong."

"I love you," she told him, finding it hard to believe her life could be so good.

"I love you, too."

SHE SAID YES. Penelope had said yes! He was going to get married. Hopefully, he'd be a father soon, too. His days were filled with all the things he loved best— Penelope, the *Amphitrite*, fishing, the sun and the wind, and all the guests who came to stay at EdgeCliff Manor.

Penelope kept everything on an even keel. She got

even the shyest novices fishing and charmed blustering old salts into admitting they still had a thing or two to learn. His job was to keep everyone talking, laughing and having a good time. Together they tended the *Amphitrite* and the house. After all these months they found a way to make every day a joy, no matter how long a list of chores they faced and even when their paying customers were cranky or jerks.

Wes helped pack up the picnic when they were done and hefted the basket to his car. He found he felt even more solicitous toward Penelope than usual. She was a strong woman who didn't need a lot of coddling, but he wanted to hover around her. To protect her. Help her.

To let everyone know he was officially her man.

Penelope was going to be his wife.

Pride filled him at the thought. He was going to be the best husband he could be. If he was granted his wish to be a father, he told himself he'd do his best in that department, too. He wouldn't force his children to be anything they didn't want to be. If they loved fishing, that would be wonderful. If they didn't, he would accommodate that, too.

They drove the short distance down from the bluffs to the Leaf. Wes parked in front of Ashbury Jewelers, the store where Noah and Sam had gotten rings for their wives. He couldn't wait to put a ring on Penelope's finger and make their engagement official.

Inside the store, a blond man built like a linebacker

sat behind the counter, bending over a tray of jewelry. He straightened as soon as they entered.

"Afternoon. Can I help you with anything?"

"We're here for an engagement ring," Wes told him. He ushered Penelope to the glass cases.

"Wonderful. I'm Lance. Let me pull out some trays for you." He pulled out a keyring and fiddled with the lock on the back of the case.

"Did I hear the words *engagement ring*?" A smaller man popped out of the back room. "That's the best kind of customer. Everyone's happy when they pick out their ring."

"I certainly am," Penelope said.

"I'm Gary. Did you know Lance designed all these? He always forgets to tell people that."

"I did know, actually. You sold rings to two of our friends." Penelope told them all about Emma and Ava and how much they adored their engagement rings. "There was nowhere else we could go, since our friends love you so much."

"That's the best kind of advertising," Gary agreed. "Go on. Try a few." He kept them laughing with stories about other customers they'd had over the years, Lance putting in a word now and then but letting Gary do most of the talking.

Meanwhile, Wes encouraged Penelope to keep trying on rings until she'd narrowed it down to three of them.

"…and it turned out he planned to propose to two

women in one day," Gary finished saying. "He figured the odds were better that one of them would say yes. Lance had to wrestle him to the ground to get our rings back. No way we're selling to a man who doesn't understand how true love works."

From the way Lance rolled his eyes, Wes figured that story had been a little embellished, but he didn't care. He understood Gary's gift for gab and for keeping a tale moving along. When Gary noticed Penelope hesitating over the three rings she hadn't put back in the tray, he said, "Turn around a moment." She did so, and he spread them out on the counter. "When you turn back, you need to instantly point to the one you want. Understand?"

Penelope nodded.

"Three… two… one. Turn around."

Penelope turned and pointed to a swoop of a ring that Wes thought was practical, in that it had no pointy bits that could be a hazard on the *Amphitrite*. It was an elegant, feminine design that reminded Wes of waves on the ocean.

"Looks perfect," Wes told her.

"It is," she agreed.

"Try it on," Lance directed.

She did, and he gave it a little tug. "Just a little loose. We can have that fixed up in no time. Can you come back in a few days?"

"Of course," Wes said.

Penelope frowned. "I wish I could have it now."

"Tell you what," Lance said. "Come back in an hour. I've got a break in my schedule."

"Are you sure?" Wes asked.

"Absolutely. We can't stand in the way of true love, right, Gary?"

"That's right."

They took care of the sale, and Wes and Penelope walked back outside.

"What should we do for an hour?" Penelope asked.

Wes could think of a lot of things, but he simply tucked her arm through his. "Let's walk on the beach."

During their hour they worked on the guest list for the wedding. They knew their friends would all pitch in to help with decorations and food.

"When do you want to hold it?" Wes asked.

Penelope made a face. "When do we even have a gap in our bookings? It could be months."

"Or it could be the third weekend of June," Wes said. "Our records say the Smith party has booked the whole house. Guess who Mr. Smith is."

"You already cleared a weekend for us? You must have been pretty confident I'd say yes." Penelope tugged on his arm, and he pulled her in close.

"I figured we'd use the weekend to get married or to figure out what the heck to do next if you turned me down."

"I'm glad we're getting married."

"Me, too."

"We're going to have to get busy preparing for the wedding, though."

"Just tell me what to do—and when to get out of the way." They'd hosted enough events already he knew the drill. "And then there's the matter of that baby you were talking about."

"We can have all kinds of fun working on that," Penelope said.

"You bet we will."

The hour passed more quickly than he expected. When they returned to the shop, Penelope's ring was ready.

"Should we go back up to the bluff so I can do this right?" he asked her.

"Do it now," she begged him. "I want to show the world that I've got you and you can never get away!"

He wanted that, too. So in front of Gary and Lance, he went down on one knee again. "Penelope Rider, do you still want to marry me?"

"Yes!"

He got up, took her hand and slid the ring gently on her finger. It fit perfectly, and she felt perfect in his arms when he pulled her close for another embrace. He kissed her, knowing he'd never be happier than when she was close to him.

"Should we show our friends?"

"That's a fantastic idea!"

"EDGECLIFF MANOR LOOKS stunning today," Emma told Penelope the morning of the wedding. "I have to admit I was surprised when you decided not to hold the ceremony on the *Amphitrite*, but I understood when I saw your guest list."

"I have a huge family," Penelope agreed, "and there would have been a riot if I left any of them out of the wedding." She and Wes had decided to hold it in the daytime, so there wouldn't be any fear of it running too late at night. EdgeCliff Manor was going to be packed. They couldn't run the risk of that many people loud and rowdy at midnight, even if their neighbors had proven to be a forgiving bunch.

"You look absolutely beautiful, Penelope," Ava said.

Penelope looked at herself in the floor-length mirror and decided she could agree with that. She wore an off-the-shoulder gown with a fitted bodice and a flowing skirt. Her hair was arranged in a fancy half updo laced with pearls. Emma and Ava were dressed in eucalyptus-green bridesmaid's gowns made of chiffon. The whole affair would be fresh and in tune with the beautiful summer day.

The flowers for the wedding were enchanting. Rows of white chairs were set up on the lawn facing a temporary pavilion at the ocean end of the lot, where the officiant would stand. Kamirah would preside over the wedding. Penelope had called on her several times on behalf of her guests after she did such a wonderful job with Olivia's wedding.

Kate, Aurora and Connor had come in and spiffed up her landscaping for the event. The women from Heaven on Earth farm had teamed up with Emma again to cater the affair. Penelope thought it was wonderful that all the people she loved had a hand in making her day special. Everywhere she looked, she saw touches that made her heart sing.

"Are you ready, Penelope?" Her mother entered the room. "Seems like most of your guests are in their seats, and I got the signal that Wes is ready."

Butterflies fluttered in her stomach at the thought of her groom waiting at the end of the aisle for her. She adjusted her veil. "I'm ready."

Her mother kissed her. "I'm so happy for you, honey. I couldn't be prouder of you, you know that, right? Your father and Uncle Dan would be proud of you, too."

"Even though I'm running fishing charters on the *Amphitrite*?"

"Especially because you are."

Getting to reconnect with her mother these past few days had been another special aspect of the occasion. Her mother was so happy in her new life. So brimming full of plans and energy. Penelope understood how that felt now and could be pleased for her mother without reservations. It helped that they'd been able to talk about what happened with Roger Atlas and the way Penelope had suffered thinking her uncle would disapprove of her choosing to fish after he'd banned her from the boat. Her mother agreed with Wes. Dan had been furious with himself, but he'd taken it out on Penelope, and that wasn't fair.

"I know Dan," she said now. "He couldn't be happier with the way you've made use of the legacy he left you. He always wanted you to follow in his footsteps. He told me that many times."

"He did?"

"Of course, honey. I'm sorry I was so involved in my own affairs I didn't see how much you were suffering this past year. I could have put your mind at rest sooner."

"That's okay." It was. Penelope had come to realize she had to take charge of her own life and her own decisions. She was too old to let her mother, father, uncle or anyone else make them for her.

"I'll go find my seat." Her mother ducked out of the room. Penelope faced her friends.

"Thank you so much for everything the two of you have done to make this the best day of my life." She held out her arms, and they came to hug her. "Cliff Street Sisters forever?" she added, reminding them of the nickname they'd given themselves when they first met.

"You know it," Ava said, hugging her fiercely. "I never dreamed life could be this good."

"Me, either," Emma said. "And I'm so glad you two

are my friends. I couldn't ask for better."

They parted, then checked themselves over one last time and lined up by the door.

"Ready?" Emma said from her place at the front.

"Ready," Penelope told her.

Emma opened the door, and they walked down the stairs.

"WHERE IS SHE?" Wes whispered to Noah.

"She's coming, don't worry."

"She's the last person who'd be a runaway bride," Sam added. "Penelope's head over heels for you."

Wes knew he was right, but his heart thumped when someone turned on the music and the "Bridal Chorus" sounded. He stood up straighter, glad that Noah and Sam, who'd become his constant surfing companions and good friends, were there with him. Grace was sitting in the first row of seats, beaming at him. These days they talked frequently and were slowly healing the wounds of their past. Now that their parents couldn't turn them against each other, they were learning they had more in common than Wes had ever dreamed possible. Abbott Enterprises was being acquired by a larger company. The closer that transaction came to being complete, the happier Grace seemed.

When Emma appeared on the deck, Noah grinned at her. Kate was holding their baby during the ceremony, and Sophia chose this moment to coo loudly. The guests chuckled as Emma beamed at her tiny daughter and she took her position on the pavilion.

Ava came next.

"There's my girl," Sam said softly, his pride easy to see.

But Wes had eyes for only his bride now as she walked toward him, a graceful vision in white. Penelope was as beautiful as he'd ever seen her, and he wondered if he would even be able to speak his vows when the time came. His throat was thick with emotion and his heart beat hard in his chest.

Penelope had chosen to walk herself down the aisle, even though Wes knew that several men in her life had offered to walk with her, including Mac, who'd come calling when their engagement was announced and apologized for his earlier behavior.

Penelope had politely declined all the offers, although he knew she was happy to be on good terms with her old family friend again.

"This is a journey I can make on my own," she'd told Wes when he asked her about it.

He thought he understood and was proud of her for speaking up for what she wanted. After today they'd always have each other to depend on, and that was what mattered most.

Now she was walking toward him, and Wes thought he had to be the happiest man alive. When she reached him, he took her hand and was as aware of her fingers within his as he was the first time he'd done so.

Together they faced Kamirah.

"Dearly Beloved," she began.

Wes hardly heard her words. He was lost in all the plans he had for the life he wanted to build with Penelope. He adored the woman who was becoming his wife—

And he'd truly found his home.

To see more books by Cora Seton, visit
www.coraseton.com.

About the Author

With over one-and-a-half million books sold, NYT, USA Today and WSJ bestselling author Cora Seton writes contemporary women's fiction and romance. She has thirty-nine novels and novellas currently set in the fictional towns of Seahaven, California and Chance Creek, Montana, with many more in the works. Cora loves the ocean, kayaking, gardening, reading, binge-watching Jane Austen movies, keeping up with the latest technology and indulging in old-fashioned pursuits. She lives on beautiful Vancouver Island with her husband, children and two cats.

Visit **www.coraseton.com** to read about new releases, contests and other cool events!

Printed in Great Britain
by Amazon

17323661R00166